SOLSTICE SONG

SOLSTICE SONG

A CHRISTMAS CAROL FOR THE 21ST CENTURY

DEIRDRE DUFFY

Divergent Ink,
Hansville, Washington

Published in the United States by Divergent Ink, Hansville, Washington.

Printed in the United States of America

www.divergentink.com

Print ISBN 978-0-692-77441-0
EPUB ISBN 978-0-692-79452-4

Library of Congress Control Number: 2016914246

Cover design and artwork by Erik Hidrup

Typesetting services by BOOKOW.COM

For the children

"There is no death. Only a change of worlds."

Chief Seattle

CONTENTS

Solstice Song

The Characters

ANDREW BLOSSOM - A Puget Sound Naval Shipyard engineer: turned defense contractor post-911. Late 50's. Compactly built and of small stature.

LYDIA BLOSSOM - Andrew's wife: died of metastatic breast cancer in 2012. Late 50's, with a stature and build similar to Andrew's.

BENJAMIN BLOSSOM - Andrew's adult son: killed in the collapse of WTC2. He was 23.

ANDREA BLOSSOM WEATHERBY - Andrew's twin sister. Elegant, and much younger-looking than Andrew.

DR. ROBERT WEATHERBY - Andrea's husband. Mid-60's.

LEAH WEATHERBY - Andrea and Robert's daughter. Born on the 11th of September, 1994. She turned 7 on the morning of 911. Age 21. She is a red-head.

PAUL GOODRICH - Leah's partner. Olive-skinned: of Syrian descent. Age 24.

C.V. GROVES - Third Officer, *SS Californian*. Age 24.

JOHN F. KENNEDY - 35th President of the United States. Assassinated on November 22, 1963. Age 46.

FALLING MAN - Unidentified African-American male, photographed falling from WTC 1 on the morning of 911. Mid-30's.

THE PLAYERS (11) - Musicians of HMS Titanic, WTC office workers, 911 first responders at the WTC Towers, wedding guests of Leah & Paul, mob members, riot police. Of varied ages, builds, genders, and ethnicities.

BENJAMIN & SHELBY GOODRICH - Leah & Paul's Children. Age 17 and 12.

The Setting

Washington, DC. Early 21st century. Andrew Blossom's penthouse, just north of Farragut Square, with a view of the Washington Monument.

The Date

September 10, 2015. Around 8 in the evening.

The Timeline

Act I - The Ghost of Conspiracy Theory Past

8:00 PM September 10, 2015: Andrew's penthouse - a dinner celebration the night before Leah's 21st birthday.

12:00 AM September 11, 2015: Andrew's penthouse - one minute after midnight: Andrew's wife Lydia visits.

1:00 AM September 11, 2015: Andrew's penthouse/deck of the SS Californian, North Atlantic - CV Groves visits (*return to April 14, 1912*).

Act II - The Ghost of Conspiracy Theory Present

1:30 AM September 11, 2015: Andrew's penthouse - Andrew dreams of young Benjamin (1985).

2:00 AM September 11, 2015: Andrew's penthouse/86th floor of WTC2 (south tower) - John F. Kennedy visits (*replay: September 11, 2001*).

Act III - The Ghost of Conspiracy Theory Future

3:00 AM, September 11, 2015: Andrew's penthouse/Black Swan Vineyard, Mount Angel, Oregon: Leah's wedding - Falling Man visits - (October 2025).

4:00 AM, September 11, 2015: Black Swan Vineyard, Leah and Paul's kitchen (November 2030).

5:00 AM, September 11, 2015: Washington Mall Tent City, Washington DC, Andrea's Tent (Winter Solstice, December 22, 2043).

6:00 AM, September 11, 2015: Andrew's penthouse.

Act I

The Ghost of
Conspiracy Theory Past

A Dinner Celebration

It is sunset, September 10, 2015. Inside Andrew Blossom's penthouse loft, the decor is spacious, modern, and starkly austere, but through a trio of French doors a sumptuous cascade of plants and shrubs on a large deck frames a view of the Washington Monument. Andrew is standing near the middle set of French doors, looking out. He is drinking a scotch on the rocks.

In the center of the room, a caterer is adjusting the flowers and table settings on a large, heavy dining table which is roughhewn and clearly quite old and quite expensive. The table setting is also visually sumptuous, almost erotic, in contrast to the rest of the room. It is set for a party of four.

On the far side of the room is the penthouse elevator: its doors and surround are an odd mix of modern, Beaux Arts, and Greek Revival styles.

As Andrew stares out at the Monument, rattling the ice in his glass, the elevator chimes and its doors glide silently open. The caterer turns to greet the arriving guests: Andrew hesitates, then quickly crosses the room as ROBERT, ANDREA, and LEAH step from the elevator.

ANDREA: Andrew! *Andrea is carrying a large salad bowl. She hugs Andrew without setting it down.*

ANDREW, *stiffly accepting Andrea's hug:* Andrea—

ROBERT, *offering a handshake to avoid hugging:* Andrew. Good to see you again.

ANDREW, *relieved:* Dr. Weatherby. Like-wise.

LEAH*:* Uncle Andy! *Leah hugs Andrew with enthusiasm.*

ANDREW: Leah. Wow. You've really grown.

LEAH: Uncle Andy. I'm almost 21. I'm not growing anymore.

ANDREW: That's right. I forget...sometimes.

There is a long pause, and an awkward silence.

ANDREA: Here's the salad, like I promised–

ANDREW: Andrea–I told you I had plenty of food–still–that's very thought-ful. *He turns to the caterer.* Charlice–will you?

The caterer takes the salad bowl from Andrea and leaves the room.

ANDREA: Servants now, Andrew?

ANDREW: Caterer, Andrea. Just for you–for tonight, I mean. We don't see each other very often, so I thought this would give us a chance to talk a little more...so someone isn't always getting up and going to the kitchen.

Robert and Andrea exchange glances: another pause.

ANDREW: Please—sit. I'll just go see what Charlice is doing—dinner should be ready—please—make yourselves at home.

Andrew exits. Andrea goes to the table, begins to rearrange the place settings, and sits down. Robert goes to make himself a drink. Leah walks to the French doors and looks out.

LEAH: I always forget how amazing the view is here.

ROBERT: And expensive.

LEAH: Yes, Dad–I know. You say that every year.

ROBERT: Just warming up for your "small talk Olympics".

LEAH: It doesn't have to be small talk, Dad. You and Mom make it that way.

ANDREA: Stop it, you two.

Andrew returns with an open bottle of wine in one hand, and his scotch in the other. The caterer is behind him, with a platter.

ANDREW: What were you saying, Robert?

ROBERT: Nothing. We were just admiring the view, as always.

Andrew stops abruptly and looks out the French doors.

ANDREW: Yes. Yes, it's very beautiful. I never tire of looking at it.

Andrew appears to lose himself for a moment in the view. His guests watch him, and try to avoid looking at each other as they wait. Abruptly, he shakes his head and turns back toward the others.

ANDREW: Leah: come on! Let's start the celebration! You're about to turn 21! A full adult–

Robert and Leah sit, Andrew pours the wine, and they toast Leah as the caterer serves. They begin to eat.

ANDREW: Tell me about this salad. *He holds up a white rubbery thing with his fork.* Is it some sort of pasta?

LEAH: It's from Keen & MaLuca, Uncle Andy.

ANDREA: Calamari caprese.

LEAH: Translation: major carbon footprint!

ROBERT: Leah.

LEAH: You know that's the whole point of Keen & MaLuca, Daddy. *To Andrew:* Mom thought you might like it. Line caught squid, from the deep trenches off the coast of Argentina.

ANDREW: You don't say.

ROBERT: It's very tasty–though I will say, the texture is a bit off-putting. Calamari always reminds me of the esophageal resections we had to do in medical school–

LEAH: Dad!

Andrew sets the squid off to the side of his plate.

LEAH: Don't worry Uncle Andy...I'm sure it's really fresh. It was probably flown in this morning. Just imagine, yesterday, that squid was part of an ecosystem deep in the cool water trenches of the southern Atlantic ...and now, it's here, on a bed of organic kale tossed with twenty-year old balsamic vinegar and triple virgin Portuguese olive oil.

ANDREW: Amazing. *Andrew picks up his scotch, sets it down without drinking.* How are things in the medical world, Robert?

ROBERT, *sawing away at the calamari, and clearly enjoying it:* Can't complain.

ANDREA: Robert's been offered a teaching fellowship. In London.

ANDREW: Teaching?

ROBERT: Yes. A recent paper of mine has generated quite a bit of attention: In-Vitro Fertilization Using Primipara Zygotes in the Multi-Para, Post-Menopausal Population: Challenges, Options, and Alternatives.

ANDREW: I see.

LEAH: Daddy is becoming famous for his ability to get rich old European women pregnant using poor young European women's eggs.

ANDREA: Leah, please–can we not get pulled into your politics for one evening?

LEAH: You mean my ethics, Mom–politics is your game.

ROBERT: Stop, Leah. *Holding his wine glass up to the light:* Very interesting wine, Andrew.

ANDREW: You think so? I'm glad to hear that–and you should enjoy it, because that's almost all there is...I bought a case of it last year. It's an extremely rare vintage...now.

ANDREA: What are you talking about, Andrew?

ANDREW: The winery–it's a Chilean wine–was sacked in one of the WTO riots a few years ago. All the vines were destroyed, as I understand it. Burned to the ground. It's all gone now.

ROBERT: What a shame.

ANDREW: Yes. The rootstock was some ancient varietal brought over from Europe at the turn of the last century, I believe. Some of the vines had been bearing for more than 80 years.

There is another long pause.

LEAH: So, Uncle Andy...how are you? I mean, how's everything?

Robert and Andrea exchange glances.

LEAH: Is business going well?

ANDREW: What? *Andrew seems distracted again.* Yes...yes it's going well. But I'm thinking about retiring.

LEAH: You always say that.

ANDREW: Yes, I know...but this time, I mean it. I'm getting old. I haven't held up as well as your mother has—*he gestures toward Andrea.* Too much work, I think.

LEAH: That must be why you never answer your phone!

ANDREA: Leah.

LEAH: I'm just talking–

ANDREW: I know–I-I- my secretary takes most of my calls...these days.

LEAH: So, I guess I should just call her, huh, when I want to talk to my favorite uncle?

Andrea is trying to catch Leah's eye; Leah ignores Andrea.

ANDREW, *trying to get with the spirit of the evening:* Oh, I'm your favorite uncle am I?

LEAH: Of course you are, Uncle Andy!

ANDREW, *laughing:* Well, it's not like I have much competition, since I'm your only uncle-

LEAH: Well, you'd still be my favorite uncle even if I had more than one uncle. *Leah leans toward Andrew with an earnest expression.* Do you remember how–when I was little–Ben would have me hide when you came home from work...

Andrew recoils slightly at the mention of Ben.

LEAH: ...and you'd sweep me out with the broom? Do you remember that, Uncle Andy?

ANDREA: Leah–

ROBERT: So, Andrew—are you going to sell?

ANDREW: What? *Shaking his head, as if trying to clear the air.* Oh...I'm not sure...I haven't really thought it through.

ROBERT: Because if you are, my group—my former group—some of the docs—they've been thinking about diversifying—

Andrea looks sharply at Robert.

ANDREA: Robert.

ROBERT, *to Andrew:* They're looking to diversify the portfolio, Andrew, that's all.

ANDREA: Into missiles?

LEAH: Missiles were 20th century, Mom. Drones are the thing now.

ROBERT: It's just a balloon—nothing more. *To Leah:* And you don't need to be so quick to judge. You and your mother have always enjoyed the lifestyle.

ANDREW: Well Robert...you should know...missile defense—and yes, Leah, drones are the 21st-century part of missile defense, since you mentioned it—it's a—a—a...it's become a tricky business.

ROBERT: How so?

ANDREW: Well...the main issue is that the Chinese are into everything these days—some people say they'll be selling us the control mechanisms for our own weapons systems next—

ANDREA: Well, that doesn't make much sense—

LEAH, *under her breath:* It's not about making sense, Mom, it's about making money—

Andrea tries to kick Leah under the table.

ANDREW: What?

ANDREA, *glaring at Leah:* Never mind, Andrew–go on.

ANDREW: Oh, well...there's no way I can compete with labor costs if that happens. But really, I don't know...one day I think it's time to stop, one day I'm full of energy.

Another awkward pause, as Andrew drifts off and again, looks out the French doors. The sky has darkened and the Monument floodlights–which have just come on–cast a garish light across the obelisk's facade.

Robert and Andrea watch Andrew for a moment, then look at each other and shift uncomfortably in their chairs, as if waiting for something to happen.

Andrew turns his gaze away from the Monument, and for a moment seems surprised to find guests at his table. He picks up his wine glass and shakes his head–as if clearing something from his mind–and turns toward Leah.

ANDREW: Leah! It's your 21st birthday tomorrow: let's talk about you. What are your plans? Are you going to take me up on my offer, now that you're done with school?

LEAH: Well, Uncle Andy, I'm glad you asked. I have some very exciting news to share with you.

Robert and Andrea exchange glances again.

ANDREW: You're getting married!

LEAH: No...I'm not getting married.

ANDREW: But you do still have that boyfriend–what's his name? The Philadelphia granola boy?

LEAH: Yes Uncle Andy...you mean Paul.

ANDREA: Paul Goodrich. His name is Goodrich, Andrew.

ANDREW: Sorry.

LEAH: And yes...he's still in the picture...but no, we're not getting married ...not right now, anyway. But we are doing something together.

Andrea and Robert exchange glances again.

ANDREW: I'm almost afraid to ask.

LEAH: It's not *that*. We're going to Ecuador together...to work on a permaculture farm.

ANDREW: A permaculture farm?

ROBERT: It's sort of like a commune, Andrew–only more organic.

ANDREA: Stop it, Robert. Let her explain it.

LEAH: Uncle Andy, permaculture is short for permanent agriculture.

ANDREW: Permanent agriculture?

LEAH: Yeah. It's about creating food systems–economies–communities– that are self-sustaining...that mimic nature.

ANDREW: Doesn't agriculture already mimic nature, Leah? Plants, dirt, water—sounds like nature to me!

Andrew laughs at his joke; the others are silent.

LEAH: No, Uncle Andy...permaculture is different. It's a philosophy as much as anything–

ANDREW: Philosophical agriculture?

ANDREA: Andrew–

ANDREW: OK–I'm sorry, Leah. Explain it to me. Please.

LEAH: It's OK, Uncle Andy. Almost everybody has that reaction at first.

ANDREW: Go ahead–I'm listening.

LEAH: Well...first of all, instead of rows and rows of the same plants, and chemically intensive processes, permaculture teaches you to think about what you're doing...as a process...

ANDREW: Like we do in missile manufacturing...an assembly line.

LEAH: Well...maybe not exactly like in missile manufacturing. Think of the forest.

ANDREW: OK.

LEAH: In a forest there's all kinds of layers. Different species. Different... uh...ecological niches.

ANDREW: OK.

LEAH: And each layer has food for the species that needs it.

ANDREW: OK.

LEAH: And when things decay they are cycled back into the–into the stock–the, uh, it's um, part of the process...and they get reused.

Leah pauses for a moment.

LEAH: ...like how leaves fall on the ground, and form the soil for the next season.

ANDREW: OK...

LEAH: Permaculture tries to–to learn from this...so instead of stripping the soil, or clear cutting a forest, or planting acres and acres of one crop, you make things more...like a forest.

ANDREA: She learned about this at school.

LEAH: At Evergreen.

ROBERT: Harvard of the West Coast, if you recall.

LEAH: Dad.

ANDREW, *perplexed:* I see. And there's money in this?

ROBERT: It's an emerging economy thing, Andy.

Andrea glares at Robert.

LEAH: Daddy thinks I'm wasting my time.

ROBERT: And our money.

LEAH: Even though I'm not spending his money.

ROBERT: As long as you don't count the four years of undergrad.

ANDREA: Will you two please stop? For one night?

ANDREW: So...will you get a teaching credential or something out of this year of work?

Andrea and Robert exchange looks again.

LEAH: No...not exactly.

ANDREW: Well, will you be able to leverage it into earnings when you come back?

LEAH: Ummm...I'm not sure...

ANDREW: Is there market demand? What's the business case?

LEAH: I'm paying my own way, Uncle Andy.

ANDREW: I see.

LEAH: And I'm–Paul and I–are fundraising too...which is why I wanted to talk to you.

ANDREW: Oh, I see. Well, I'm giving you a birthday present–cash, as always. It's a little heftier this year–in honor of graduating and turning 21. That should help.

LEAH: I'm sure it will, Uncle Andy–thank you–and just so you know, my trip is already funded. That's not what I'm talking about. *Leah hesitates:* It's your job offer: I'd like to propose an alternative.

ANDREW: An alternative job?

LEAH, *more confident:* No...not exactly. A grant. I'd like you to consider giving Paul and me a grant.

Andrea and Robert exchange looks again.

ANDREW: A grant?

LEAH: Yes. A pay-it-forward grant. For start-up capital.

ANDREW: A grant? As in free money, no strings attached?

LEAH: No Uncle Andy–not free money. We'd write a proposal–we'd work the details out with you...for how it would work. *Leah glances quickly at her parents, then turns back toward Andrew:* Paul and I want to start a for-profit non-profit.

ANDREW: A for-profit non-profit?

LEAH: Yes...it's a business enterprise, Uncle Andy. Our ultimate goal is empowering people to work to live...rather than live to work.

Andrea and Robert are watching Andrew very closely.

ANDREW: This doesn't make any sense to me–Robert?

ROBERT: It's a little hard to understand at first, Andy—it's best if you don't over-think it.

ANDREW: OK...so, Leah...what sort of non-profit, for-profit business enterprise do you and Paul have in mind, exactly?

LEAH: Well...we won't have the details until we come back, of course...but we're hoping to teach permaculture skills to other people. And to help them create business ventures that directly benefit them and their producers, locally...rather than benefiting big business.

ANDREW: And what's wrong with big business?

ANDREA: Nothing Andrew—what Leah means is—

ROBERT: Andrea—let Leah handle it.

LEAH: Uncle Andy—

ANDREW: Let me see if I've got this right...you and Paul are planning to spend a year on a dirt farm in some third world country—

ANDREA: Developing country, Andrew—

ANDREW: OK—developing country, uh, doing unpaid labor. And when you come back, you're planning to get grants to teach other people the skills they need so they too can NOT make money?

ANDREA: Andrew!

ANDREW: Do I have that right?

ROBERT: Andrea—

LEAH: Yes. No—it's not how it sounds, Uncle Andy—I mean, I don't know exactly how it's going to look, or work. I don't think that way about it. I'm—Paul and I—we—we're trying to figure out how to live in this world. It's not the same as it was when you were young. It's not just about jobs, or money. It's about the entire structure of our economy–

ANDREW, *trying not to show his irritation:* I have no idea what that means. And it seems to me, Leah, that it is about jobs and money. College is over. You've had your fun–and I'm sure you discovered some passions in school–that's natural–but now you need to earn a living.

LEAH: No–look Uncle Andy–Paul and I–are getting skills. When we're done with our fellowship, we're going to come back and develop a cooperative enterprise...somehow. We're going to do it. This is what we want. And it will make money...it just won't make money for giant, multinational corporations. *Leah becomes very animated:* It isn't meant to. It's about...cooperation. It's about taking care of the places we live in. It's about knowing your neighbors–the plants and animals ...and the people.

ANDREW: A cooperative enterprise? That sounds like some sort of social-ism, Leah.

ANDREA: No Andrew, it isn't–

LEAH: Mom, let me–Uncle Andy–what we're trying to do–it isn't going to fit any of your mental models–

ANDREW: My mental models?

LEAH: It's not about getting a McJob–

ANDREW: A McJob? What the hell is a McJob?

LEAH: ...or about capitalism or socialism, or any of the isms–

ANDREW: Isms...you mean, like patriotism?

ANDREA: Andrew, I swear if you–

ROBERT: It's a figure of speech Andrew, don't take it personally–

LEAH: Permaculture isn't any kind of ism, Uncle Andy...and it's growing all over the world. And we've decided we want to be a part of it. Paul and I...we want to grow things...and restore the ecology...and help make the world more beautiful...instead of making it uglier.

ANDREW: Are you implying that my offer is to make things uglier, Leah?

LEAH: No, Uncle Andy...that's not what I mean...I mean, what we're trying, what we're about...well...we're...we're...we're social entrepreneurs!

ANDREW: Social entrepreneurs.

LEAH: Yes, Uncle Andy. Social entrepreneurs.

ANDREW: I see.

Andrew's face is red, and he has become very still. He slowly reaches for his scotch, then raises it quickly, knocking back his drink.

Robert and Andrea are watching Andrew intently.

ANDREW: Well–you have certainly thought this out, Leah.

LEAH, *beaming, oblivious to Andrew's body language:* Thanks Uncle Andy. We have actually–we already have a challenge grant from the Washington Peace Coalition–

ROBERT: Leah–

LEAH: ...and if we can raise twenty-thousand dollars, they'll match it.

Robert shakes his head, tries to catch Leah's eye. She ignores him.

ANDREW, *a bit hostile:* Washington Peace Coalition. That sounds like some sort of lobbyist group for the other Washington.

ANDREA: It *is* a lobbyist group for the other Washington, Andrew.

ROBERT: Leah–

LEAH: Uncle Andy...I really wish you could glimpse our vision. Paul and I, and some of our classmates from Evergreen....well, this is a long way off but–

ROBERT, *still trying to catch Leah's eye:* Then maybe you should wait to talk about it, Leah–

LEAH: ...we want to create an institute, a place where we can bring inner city youth, kids that are in foster care, people who aren't in the workforce anymore...and we want to teach them about permaculture–it's a movement, Uncle Andy–a craft revival–organic gardening, breadmaking, cheese-making, raising animals, building earth-sheltered housing, passive solar design, re-creating community...there's so much that needs to be done...and when we come back, we're going to need seed money. So...will you think about it at least–about contributing, when I come back?

There's a long silence at the table. Andrea and Robert look at each other, and at Leah. Leah looks at Andrew.

Andrew turns to look out at the Washington Monument again. The sky is now completely dark, and at the Monument's pinnacle, a pair of red lights are blinking steadily.

Andrew watches the lights for a moment, and when he speaks again his voice is far away.

ANDREW: It's a dangerous world, Leah.

ANDREA: Andrew–

Andrew turns back into the room again, to face his guests. He leans forward toward Leah.

ANDREW: You're passionate, Leah. I get that. But the world–I – plants, and dirt, and running around in your shirt sleeves teaching some kind of–well–it sounds like welfare to me, Leah–

ANDREA: Here we go–

ANDREW: A way for people to avoid working for a living–

LEAH: It's not, Uncle Andy–

ANDREW: Or some sort of put down of all the people in this country who've been willing to sacrifice themselves for the greater good–

ANDREA: Andrew.

ANDREW, *raises his hand, leans back, crosses his arms:* No–wait–let me have my say now. I'm sorry, Leah–but your idea, well, it's compelling to be sure...but it's not something I'm willing to throw my money at. Jobs and industry, Leah–that's where I want to do good–

LEAH: This is jobs and industry, Uncle Andy.

ROBERT: Stop, Leah. He just gave you his answer.

ANDREA: She gets a little carried away, Andrew.

LEAH: Stop patronizing me.

ROBERT: You need to learn when to stop. Make the ask, and when someone says no, it means no. You don't keep pushing–no matter what they taught you at Evergreen.

LEAH: What they taught me at Evergreen was how to think. And how to stand up for what I think.

ANDREW, *his voice condescending, with just a hint of an edge:* Sometimes it's not about what we think.

LEAH: Really? Then what is it about?

ANDREW: It's about values. And about not compromising them.

LEAH: Oh, really. *Leah sits back in her chair and pauses for a moment. When she speaks again, her voice is lower and her gaze unwavering.* And that's something you and my parents know about, right?

ANDREW: What?

LEAH: Like you didn't compromise your values? After Ben died?

Andrew visibly recoils at the mention of Ben's death–as if he has been struck.

ANDREA: Leah!

Andrew places both his hands on the edge of the table and grips, white-knuckled.

ANDREW: What are you talking about, Leah?

Robert and Andrea are both shaking their heads at Leah: Leah continues to ignore them both.

LEAH: If Ben were here, he'd support what I'm doing. And he'd want you to support this–

ANDREA: Oh my god. Leah, please.

LEAH: No–I've had enough. You two don't support me–I know–you just don't get it–

Andrew appears paralyzed by Leah's words: he opens and closes his mouth several times without speaking.

ANDREW, *breathy, soft, and halting, with great effort:* What do you mean, if Ben were here? Ben isn't here. What kind of a comment is that?

ROBERT: Andrew...I'm sorry–she shouldn't have said that–

LEAH: Don't apologize for me! I can speak for myself–we're always walking on eggshells around him, every damn year, every year–

ANDREW, *whispering:* Walking on eggshells around who?

LEAH: I try to pretend it's OK to come here and eat cake and ice cream and we never talk about him–

ANDREA, *to Robert:* I told you she'd do this–

LEAH: Stop it Mom! It's my birthday–and we NEVER talk about him. Why can't we just talk about him? Why does he have to be off limits?

Andrew slams his hands on the table, then stares at them as if they are not his.

ANDREW: Stop talking about Benjamin!

ROBERT: Andrew–no one is trying–Leah is just passionate–

Andrew continues to stare at his hands. He again appears frozen, unable to move.

LEAH: Stop putting words in my mouth, Dad–

ANDREA: Leah, stop now or we're going to leave–

LEAH: Fine! Let's leave! *She starts to get up from the table.* Uncle Andy–I'm not trying to manipulate you. I'm trying to show you who I am. I have something I want to do, and Bennie is a part of it–

ANDREW, *whispering, still staring at his hands and sitting rigid in his chair:* Benjamin is not a part of anything you're doing–

LEAH: Yes, he is Uncle Andy–he *is* a part of it–even if you don't see it. He is. He always has been.

ANDREW, *covering his ears with his hands:* Enough. That's enough.

ROBERT, *standing up and throwing his napkin down onto the table:* Andrew– I'm sorry–we've upset you. This was a bad idea–Leah–no–don't say anything more. Andrew–it wasn't intentional–

Robert takes Leah by the elbow, and walks her to the elevator. They get in and as the doors start to close, Leah stops them. She steps out, pulling away from Robert.

LEAH: Uncle Andy...I was a little girl when Bennie died.

ROBERT, *from within the elevator:* Leah!

LEAH: He died on my birthday, Uncle Andy.

ANDREA: Leah, will you please!

LEAH, *tearful:* All those people, they died on my birthday–

ROBERT: Leah–

LEAH: And if Ben were here–if he'd survived–I know he'd support me– because he'd be living in my world, not yours. You don't want to hear it, because you know it's true–

ROBERT: Leah–get in the elevator now!

LEAH: I'm not going to be part of the death machine Uncle Andy–

ANDREA: Leah!

LEAH: And I'd rather live in the dirt in Ecuador than live here the way you do–and the way my parents do–

ROBERT, *grabbing Leah and pulling her into the elevator:* GET IN NOW!

LEAH, *as the elevator doors close:* 911 was an inside job, Uncle Andy! And you need to deal with it!

Andrew remains frozen in his chair. His sister starts to reach out to touch his hand, then she stops, gets up, and goes to the elevator herself.

As Andrea waits for the elevator to return, the caterer enters the room and begins to clear the dishes. The elevator returns and the doors glide open with a soft chime.

Andrea turns to look at her brother: he continues to sit with his head in his hands, focused on the table in front of him.

Andrea departs, the caterer leaves the room, and Andrew remains sitting at the table, as the floodlights on the Washington Monument gradually change from yellow to orange to blue, then fade altogether.

* * *

Andrew's Wife Lydia Visits

It is midnight, and Andrew is sleeping. The master bedroom suite, like the main loft, is austere, except for a primitive bureau and chair, and a massive roughhewn bed, dressed in expensive but simple linens.

Andrew's clothes are hung over the back of the chair, and through a single set of French doors, the Washington Monument can be seen—now flooded in yellow-white light and patterned with a shadowy grid.

In the main loft area, the elevator chimes, and the doors can be heard opening and closing. A moment later, LYDIA enters the bedroom. Approximately the same age, height, and build as Andrew, she is dressed in an elegant grey cashmere dress and wears her hair in a chic silver bob. A pair of reading glasses are draped around her neck, hung from a colorful crystal-studded chain.

Lydia stops at the foot of the bed and runs her hands lightly over the blankets as she looks at Andrew, and then around the room. She goes to the closet, gets out a hanger, and walks to the chair. She picks up Andrew's shirt, shakes it out and places it on the hanger; she does the same with the trousers.

After hanging the clothes up in the closet, Lydia looks around again. She spots the socks under the bed and picks them up. She pulls the toes out, smoothing them, and sets them neatly on the dresser, one on top of the other. Then she goes to the foot of the bed, sits down, and wiggles Andrew's feet through the blankets.

LYDIA, *softly:* Andrew.

Andrew doesn't respond.

LYDIA, *slightly louder:* Andrew.

Lydia wiggles Andrew's feet again.

LYDIA: Andrew–wake up.

ANDREW, *barely responds:* Mmmmmmmmmm.

Lydia picks up a pill bottle from the nightstand. She puts on her reading glasses and studies the label.

LYDIA: Damn it, Andrew.

Lydia puts the bottle back down and takes Andrew's shoulders with her hands: she pulls him over onto his back, grabs both his shoulders, and shakes.

LYDIA: Andrew: wake up!

Andrew is not responsive. Lydia sighs, stands up, leans over him, takes a deep breath, and shouts.

LYDIA: ANDDDDDDDDDD-RRRRRRREW!!!!

Andrew leaps out of bed and runs to the French doors.

ANDREW: What? What is it? Is it Ben? What happened?

Lydia smooths the blankets out, and sits down on the bed.

LYDIA: You always were such a heavy sleeper, Andrew. *She smiles at Andrew.* I see that hasn't changed.

ANDREW: Lydia?

Andrew remains by the French doors, with his hand on the door handle.

LYDIA: Andrew.

ANDREW: *Andrew removes his hand from the door handle, and turns to look more closely at Lydia.* Lydia—

LYDIA: Andrew.

ANDREW: Lydia.

LYDIA: Yes, Andrew–it's really me. How many times are you going to repeat my name?

ANDREW, *shaking his head and pressing on his temples:* What is this? Am I dreaming?

LYDIA: Well, you're not *dead*--that's for certain.

ANDREW, *to himself:* It's the pills. It must be the pills. *Andrew turns toward the French doors; he looks out at the Monument.* When I look back she'll be gone.

LYDIA: No I won't. *Lydia continues to sit on the bed and to run her hands over the blankets.* Cashmere. And in army surplus colors. That's taking the homeland security thing a little far, don't you think?

ANDREW, *turning his gaze back toward Lydia and smiling slightly:* I like that blanket: it's very warm. *Andrew takes a step toward the bed.* Besides–it reminds me of you.

LYDIA: Is that so?

ANDREW: Yes. I thought you would like the color.

LYDIA: Well. Yes.

Andrew crosses the room and stands at the foot of the bed.

ANDREW: Lydia.

LYDIA: Andrew.

ANDREW: It's really you.

LYDIA: I'm afraid so.

ANDREW: What are you doing here?

LYDIA: I came to check up on you.

Andrew looks perplexed. He takes a step back.

LYDIA: Oh lighten up, Andrew–I'm only staying for a few minutes.

A hint of a smile crosses Andrew's face again.

ANDREW: Lydia?

LYDIA: Yes, Andrew?

ANDREW: May I sit next to you?

Lydia smiles faintly and again runs her hands over the blankets. Then she looks away from Andrew, off into the distance.

LYDIA: Do you know–just now–you sounded exactly the way you did the first time we met. Almost the same words...with the same diffidence in your voice.

ANDREW: Yes. I remember.

LYDIA: Do you?

ANDREW: Yes. You were sitting at that corner table–at the Trillium Cafe.

LYDIA: That's right-at school.

ANDREW: I remember. The sunlight was coming in–and you were–

Andrew stops talking. He reaches out and puts his hand on the blanket. Lydia turns to look at him.

ANDREW: It's just that...well...I'm just not sure if I should sit next to you.

LYDIA: It's not contagious, Andrew.

Andrew continues to stand at the foot of the bed.

LYDIA, *patting the mattress*: Sit, Andrew. Sit.

Andrew sits beside Lydia. As he does, the elevator chimes softly. Andrew looks toward the sound.

LYDIA: It's for me, Andrew–don't worry about it.

Andrew studies Lydia's face.

ANDREW: Lydia.

LYDIA: Andrew.

ANDREW: You look so–

Andrew pauses, continuing to look at Lydia's face, as if he is not quite sure it is her.

LYDIA: What? Alive?

ANDREW: I was going to say...real.

LYDIA: I am real, Andrew. As real as ever.

Lydia leans against Andrew, and they both close their eyes for a moment. The elevator chimes softly again, and Lydia sits up abruptly.

LYDIA: I have something to tell you, Andrew. And I only have a minute.

ANDREW: A minute? What do you mean?

The elevator chimes again–slightly louder.

LYDIA: Damn. Damn–yes, I'm coming—

ANDREW: What Lydia? What is it?

LYDIA: Andrew, listen–

ANDREW: I'm listening–what?

LYDIA: Andrew...this is really important...you might think–I mean, I look alive, but–well, you know, I'm not. You know—*she smiles sadly at Andrew.* I'm dead, Andrew. I'm dead.

Andrew continues to study Lydia's face intently.

ANDREW, *whispering:* I know, Lydia. I know.

LYDIA: But here's the thing–

The elevator chimes again–louder and more insistent.

LYDIA: –you're not.

ANDREW: I'm not what?

LYDIA: You're not dead, Andrew. Not yet. You still have time.

ANDREW: Lydia–you're not making any sense.

LYDIA: I know–I know. This is harder than I thought it would be.

ANDREW: What is?

LYDIA: Explaining to you–

ANDREW: Explaining what?

LYDIA: Why I'm here.

ANDREW: Why you're here?

LYDIA: Stop parroting me!

ANDREW: Sorry.

Andrew leans toward Lydia to kiss her hair: Lydia closes her eyes and sighs.

LYDIA: Oh, Andrew.

ANDREW: Yes, Lydia?

LYDIA: Do you remember what it was like when we were young? When Ben was little?

Andrew pauses for a moment, as if he is going to freeze. Then he leans in again, closes his eyes, and deeply inhales the scent of Lydia's hair.

ANDREW, *whispering:* I remember I was happy, Lydia. I remember we were happy. *Andrew sits up and opens his eyes.* That was a long time ago.

LYDIA: Time is a relative thing, Andrew.

ANDREW: What's that supposed to mean?

LYDIA: Just that.

The elevator chimes again—this time, a double chime.

LYDIA: Damn. *Lydia stands up, walks to the bureau and picks up the socks.* Andrew—I don't have the luxury of time...and I can't explain the details to you...but you've gone down the wrong path...and things are— well, they're worse than we thought—

ANDREW: I know you always had a different point of view, Lydia, but—

LYDIA: Shhh. They're worse than I thought, too...and I used to think we'd find the time to set things right...that we'd figure it out, do our part as older people...especially after Ben died. But then-

ANDREW: But then you got sick, Lydia. I know.

LYDIA: Yes. And then I got sick, and, well...tonight's your chance, Andrew.

ANDREW: My chance? For what?

LYDIA, *twisting the socks:* Your chance to get it right. To try to–to start to–make things right.

ANDREW: To make what right, Lydia? I don't understand.

LYDIA: Oh Andrew.

ANDREW, *confused:* Lydia–what is it you're trying to say? I'm a good man.

LYDIA: You are.

ANDREW: I am-I was–a–a good husband.

LYDIA: You were. You are.

ANDREW: And I was a good father–after Ben–I

LYDIA: Andrew–

ANDREW: I did my duty, Lydia. After Ben–I–I–

Still sitting on the bed, Andrew leans forward and looks down at the floor. He covers his face with his hands and shakes his head slowly.

ANDREW, *whispering:* I did what I could after that, Lydia. You know I did.

LYDIA: Andrew –

ANDREW: What?

Lydia starts to reach out toward Andrew, then stops herself.

LYDIA: Andrew. I know. But that's the problem.

The elevator chimes again, several chimes in random sequence–insistently. Lydia turns toward the door, then she turns back.

LYDIA: Andrew–I have to go–but I need you to hear something. I need you to understand. It took a lot of effort to put this together–

ANDREW: Put what together?

LYDIA: I want you to know–tonight, some friends of mine–new friends–will be coming to see you.

ANDREW: New friends of yours?

LYDIA: Shh. Yes. New friends. And this is really important, OK? I need you to do something, something really, really hard.

ANDREW: What, Lydia?

LYDIA: Andrew. *Lydia sets the socks down on the edge of the bed.* Will you please try to turn off the Fox News Network bullshit in your head for one night, and listen to what they have to say?

ANDREW: Oh Lydia.

LYDIA: Will you do that for me? Please?

ANDREW: But Lydia–I have no idea what you are talking about.

LYDIA: Of course you don't, dear: you've made a career out of being pig-headed. Give it a try, will you? For me? For Ben?

The elevator chimes again, three times in sequence. Lydia goes quickly to Andrew, kisses him lightly on the cheek; then she steps back, and rubs the kiss off with her fingertips.

LYDIA: And put your socks on, Andrew. You're going to need them.

Andrew watches as Lydia walks out of the bedroom. The elevator doors can be heard opening, then closing.

After she leaves, Andrew sits on the bed for a few minutes, then puts on his socks. He picks up the pill bottle on the nightstand, shakes out a few more pills and swallows them dry. He falls back on the bed, into another deep sleep.

Outside, the Washington Monument fades away, and the blue lights of the Twin Towers flare up, then disappear, leaving the sky completely dark.

* * *

CV Groves Visits

It is now 1:00 a.m. As Andrew sleeps, a strange fog begins to seep in through the French doors of the master suite. As the fog moves in, the walls and the French doors fade away, and a railing appears around the perimeter of the bedroom, transforming it into the shelter deck of a merchant ship.

The floor beneath Andrew's bed begins to roll gently, and the night becomes darker. Ice begins to form on the ship's railing. In the midst of these changes, Andrew continues to sleep, his breath frosting above the blankets.

The elevator chimes softly; again its doors can be heard opening and closing. A moment later, CV GROVES enters the room. Dressed in a peacoat, ear muffs, officer's cap, and heavy gloves, he passes by Andrew, and takes up watch beside the ship's railing.

The bedroom door fades away, the wind comes up, and the fog dissipates, revealing a clear, moonless, star-covered night sky above the deck of a now motionless and ice-encrusted ship.

Groves stamps his feet, pulls his collar up closer against the arctic air, removes his gloves, and lights a cigarette. After putting his gloves back on, he resumes his stance and continues to stare out at the water.

The wind dies down, and all that can be heard is the creaking of ice against the hull of the ship. When Groves is nearly finished smoking his cigarette, he walks to Andrew's bed, pulls the bedding off, drops it onto the deck, then returns to the railing to resume his watch.

Andrew begins to toss in the cold air. With his eyes still closed, he reaches around the bed, searching for his blankets. Failing to find them, he opens his eyes, then sits up.

ANDREW: Jesus—why the hell is it so cold in here? *He looks around.* What the—

Andrew gets out of bed: as he does, the bed disappears into shadow. Andrew picks up the grey blanket from the deck of the ship and drapes it over his shoulders. He approaches Groves.

ANDREW: Who the hell are you? And what the hell are you doing in my bedroom?

Groves continues to stare out toward the horizon.

GROVES: Good evening, sir. CV Groves, Third Officer, SS Californian.

Groves takes one last drag on his cigarette, drops it onto the deck and grinds it out with his foot. He blows the smoke out over the railing.

GROVES: And I'm not in your bedroom, sir—you're on my ship, as it were. Middle of the North Atlantic. Mid-April.

ANDREW: The SS Californian?

GROVES: That's right sir. SS Californian.

ANDREW: A cruise ship? In the middle of winter?

Andrew's teeth start to chatter. He pulls the blanket more tightly over his shoulders.

GROVES: Merchant ship. Leyland line.

Andrew looks over the railing.

ANDREW: We're not moving.

GROVES: No sir. She's caught in the pack ice. A narrow call too. We're
here till morning–till it's light enough to see our way.

*Andrew walks around to the other side of Groves. Groves continues to look out
at the water.*

ANDREW: You're not real.

GROVES: She said you'd be difficult.

ANDREW: Who?

GROVES: The missus.

ANDREW: The missus?

GROVES: That's right-the missus.

ANDREW: Lydia.

GROVES: That's right.

ANDREW: She said I'd be difficult.

GROVES: She did.

ANDREW: Really? In what way?

*Groves takes off his gloves and gets out another cigarette. He hangs it in his
mouth and puts his gloves back on.*

GROVES: Oh, I expect she was referring to the usual late twentieth century afflictions: media bias, reactivity, intellectual laziness, political
correctness–

ANDREW: I am NOT politically correct. Lydia would NEVER say that
about me.

GROVES: You see–right there–you've just done it. I didn't say she said you
were politically correct. I said she said you'd be difficult. *Groves gets*

out his matches and leans forward to light his cigarette. The list of ways was my own.

ANDREW: And how was I supposed to know that?

GROVES: You could ask. Start by checking your assumptions, and by not jumping so quick to conclusions–you Americans have a real problem with that–always have.

ANDREW: I have no idea what you're talking about.

GROVES: Shhhh–stop talking–look. Out there.

ANDREW: What?

GROVES: She's to our south, heading west.

ANDREW, *squinting and trying to follow Groves' gaze:* Uh....

GROVES: Do you see her?

ANDREW: I see some lights...moving...on the horizon.

GROVES: That's right. That's her. Now–keep watching. Watch closely.

They watch for a minute: Groves with ease, Andrew with effort. Andrew's face changes: he seems confused and starts to turn toward Groves.

GROVES: No–don't turn–don't look away. Tell me what you see–but don't look away.

ANDREW: Uh–I'm not sure. I think the lights–I think they just flashed–or they disappeared for a moment, then came back–like something got in front of them, or someone threw a switch or something–

Without taking his eyes off the horizon, Groves drops his cigarette, grinds it out, and takes a watch out of his pocket. He hands the watch to Andrew.

GROVES: Note the time.

ANDREW: 1140.

GROVES: 2340.

ANDREW: Right.

GROVES: And the date.

ANDREW: What?

GROVES: The date. What's the date. For the log.

ANDREW: Uh...September 10–I mean 11. I think.

GROVES: Guess again.

ANDREW: What?

GROVES: Guess again. The date.

ANDREW: I have no idea.

GROVES: April 14, 1912.

ANDREW: April 14, 1912?

GROVES: Soon to be April 15, 1912.

Groves removes a log book from within the inside flap of his coat. He hands it to Andrew.

GROVES: Note the time in the log.

ANDREW: What?

GROVES: Write down the time in the log, please. The date. And the time.

ANDREW, *opening the log and flipping through it:* There's no place to write. It's already full.

GROVES: Exactly.

ANDREW: I don't understand.

Groves adjusts his coat, pulls his earmuffs down over the bottom of his ears. Andrew pulls the blanket more tightly around his body.

ANDREW: My god, it's cold out here.

GROVES, *nodding:* One of the coldest nights of the year.

ANDREW: I'm glad I wore my socks.

GROVES: And calm. And absolutely clear. Sea like a looking glass...sky like a cathedral. *He takes his eyes off the horizon, and looks up at the sky overhead.* Everyone should see a sky like this at least once in their lives, I think. *He sighs as he gazes at the stars.* I thought I'd seen a night sky...until I joined the merchant navy. I'll never forget my first night watch on the deck of a seagoing vessel. I wept like a baby–a baby–the first time I saw them. *Reluctantly, Groves returns his gaze to the horizon.*

ANDREW: Saw who?

GROVES: The stars, man! The stars!

Andrew looks up at the night sky, then back at Groves.

ANDREW: Really.

GROVES: Shh. Keep your eyes on the horizon. Now what do you see?

ANDREW: Uh...I...don't think she's moving any more. Or if she is, she's moving a lot slower.

The elevator chimes softly. Groves notices it. Andrew does not.

GROVES, *to Andrew:* Are you sure?

ANDREW: What?

GROVES: Are you sure? That she isn't moving any more?

ANDREW: Yes. No. I'm not sure. *Andrew turns to look at Groves.* Do you
know something I don't know?

GROVES: Keep watching.

A flash occurs in the sky.

ANDREW: Oh! That was–I think I just saw something–

Groves is very still, looking out, his eyes locked on the horizon.

ANDREW: Did you see that?

GROVES: See what?

ANDREW: That–what I just saw–

GROVES: And what did you see then?

ANDREW: Uh–I'm not sure. But I think I saw a–a–light–a flare–a...maybe
a rocket of some sort.

GROVES: A flare? A rocket? Really?

ANDREW: Yes–just now. Didn't you see it?

GROVES: What color was it?

ANDREW: What?

GROVES: What color was it?

ANDREW: I don't know. Uh–I think maybe–

GROVES: Come on man! Be forceful–what color was it? White? Blue?
Red?

ANDREW: Uh–white. I think.

GROVES, *to himself:* White he thinks–white. Why white? Because that was one of the choices I gave him...and we all know that's the kind of tests we get in life–multiple choice, answers laid out in front of you, no thought required–

ANDREW: What the hell are you talking about? Tests? Multiple choice? *Andrew looks to the horizon then back at Groves.* What is going on here? Why are you here? *He pauses, then adds:* Why am I here?

The elevator chimes faintly.

GROVES: Alright sir–we're almost out of time. So let's see if you can put the pieces together, shall we?

ANDREW: Pieces of what?

GROVES: The pieces of this puzzle...which you don't seem to understand. *Groves readjusts his collar, stamps his feet, and shivers.* Let's see if I can help you get a handle on this situation–to understand the context, if you will.

ANDREW: The situation? The context?

GROVES: Yes. The situation. The context. This situation.

Andrew looks blankly at Groves.

GROVES: Come on, will you?! You're an engineer, aren't you–an educated man. Do I have to spell it out for you?

ANDREW: Apparently.

GROVES, *sighing:* Alright then. Where are we?

ANDREW: We're at sea.

GROVES: Where at sea?

ANDREW: Uh...the North Atlantic.

GROVES: That's right. We're in the North Atlantic, caught in the pack ice, on April 14, 1912. And we're standing watch, you and me, on the shelter deck of the SS Californian. And at half-past 2300 hours–1130 pm to you civilians–we see another steamer–and by my sights a much larger one–in our vicinity, to our south, traveling west, toward New York. And then, around 2340–1140 pm–we see some lights flash, and that steamer, she seems to stop moving, a bit of time passes, and then ...let's see...a bit after midnight...what was it you just saw?

ANDREW: I saw some sort of ...of...rocket.

GROVES: Right. Now–look again. Just be patient. Let's just stand here a while, looking out at that horizon, and we'll let your mind give you the answer.

Groves resumes his stance in front of the railing, his eyes fixed steadily on the horizon. Andrew does the same. A minute passes, during which Andrew looks at Groves, then back out to the horizon, then back at Groves again. Gradually, Andrew's expression changes from one of confusion to one of tentative recognition.

ANDREW: You telling me that's the Titanic out there?

Groves lights another cigarette. The elevator chimes again–this time twice.

ANDREW: You telling me you watched the Titanic sink?

Groves says nothing.

ANDREW: You telling me that–

Andrew stops–looks out again then back at Groves.

ANDREW: Explain that to me.

Groves still says nothing.

ANDREW: Hey. Answer me! What is this? Is this real? Did this happen?

GROVES: Oh, it happened alright.

ANDREW: You watched the Titanic sink? You were close enough to see her–and you watched her sink?

GROVES: Some might say we did, sir–from 10, 11 nautical miles... *Groves shrugs.* But some might say we didn't.

ANDREW: But why? You could've done something. All those people. They were right there? And you didn't do anything? Is–is–is that what you're saying?

GROVES: Well now, sir–I wouldn't take it that far–

ANDREW: Well I would–if it's true–if what you say is true–

GROVES: It's more complicated than that.

ANDREW: In what way? It seems pretty straightforward to me–

The sky flashes again.

ANDREW: Oh–there's another rocket!

GROVES: And what color was that one? Did you see?

ANDREW: White. I think it was white.

GROVES: Are you sure?

ANDREW: What difference does it make? *Andrew starts to pace: he slips on the icy deck and catches himself on the railing.* It's got to be a distress rocket–you've got to tell someone–wake the captain–why didn't you wake the captain?

GROVES: What makes you think we didn't wake the captain? Good god man!

ANDREW: And what's with the business of the rockets? Lives are at stake here–

The elevator chimes again–this time, louder.

GROVES: Well, that's the key, you see. Those rockets, that is. Because when you go to the captain, and you wake him up–and he's not a nice person, if you know what I mean–he's going to want to know about those rockets, see? So you better be sure about the color. Because it's going to matter. The color is key.

ANDREW: White then. Call them white.

GROVES, *shaking his head:* Well, don't you know? History does have a way of repeating, doesn't it.

ANDREW: What do you mean?

GROVES: We called them as we saw them–just as you did now. And that was all we could do–because you know, to us it was hard to tell–I mean, look at this–sky like a wheel, sea like a plate of glass, and God's breath–nothing more, blowing the ice–the whole armada of it–south. It was like watching giants glide across a valley...something you see once in a lifetime, if ever. *Groves pauses and looks up at the stars again, as if he is searching for something.* So white we called it, and the captain said keep signaling them–and so we did. And we tried to figure it out–

ANDREW: So you did?

GROVES: Did what?

ANDREW: Watch her sink?

GROVES: No. We didn't watch her sink. Some watched her move, some watched lights, some saw rockets, and we talked amongst ourselves, that night and for years after. But at that point in time, we didn't know what we were seeing.

ANDREW: But—

GROVES: And that's the difference between then and now. In the moments between her hitting the iceberg and her sinking, we only had our senses to guide us. And a leader we neither liked nor trusted.

Andrew turns to look out at the horizon again, then back at Groves.

ANDREW: So you said nothing?

GROVES: You know her story.

ANDREW: Yes...but you said nothing?

GROVES: Well, that's the heart of it, isn't it? What we did or didn't do. What we did or didn't say. Of course we didn't say nothing. But in New York, pressure was put on us, ways of asking questions were used, not to help us describe what we saw–or how it related to the Titanic–but to confuse.

ANDREW: So you said nothing?

GROVES: No, we didn't say nothing. But what we said was twisted–and we were kept apart, talked to separately, questioned till we questioned ourselves.

ANDREW: And then what?

GROVES: Oh, our captain was reprimanded–but the whole thing was downplayed–

ANDREW: And?

GROVES: People wanted to move on. Move on, they said, move on.

ANDREW: So that's it, then? You moved on.

GROVES: No–I didn't move on. We–the crew–didn't move on. They moved on–the officials, the public, the journalists. Even those crew members who thought they'd moved on didn't–not really. For us– see, we were there–we knew what we'd experienced–but we couldn't unravel the mystery of it, not in words anyway. So, moving on wasn't so easy. *Groves walks along the deck, running his hand along the rail. As he does, ice breaks off and falls onto the deck, shattering.* After something like that, you go home, and you let it stew–and later, when we tried to talk about it-to ourselves, even, to tell the truth about what hap- pened so we could put it to rest properly–we were told–and this was long after the captain had been reprimanded–long after the event– we were told that we were trying to create some kind of conspiracy where there was none...*Groves turns to look sharply at Andrew.* And you know, you hear that enough, well...it does things to your mind.

ANDREW: What does?

GROVES: Finding out that reality isn't always made by the ones who live something. *Groves takes off his cap, and turns to look out at the horizon again.* So down the memory hole she went...just like the Titanic... to the bottom of the North Atlantic. And after that, for those of us who saw, and those of us who knew...well...we each had a choice to make.

ANDREW: A choice? What sort of choice?

The elevator chimes three times in short sequence, and the fog begins to seep in again through the French doors, rapidly obscuring the sky and the shelter deck.

GROVES: Well, now–that's something you'll need to figure out for yourself, Mr. Blossom. Good evening, sir.

ANDREW: I don't understand. What the hell does this have to do with me?

Groves disappears into the fog. The elevator doors can be heard opening and closing, as the wind comes up again and blows Andrew's blanket off.

The fog dissipates, and Andrew is back in his bedroom, standing alone in the center of the room: outside the French doors, the moon has risen behind the Washington Monument, casting a long shadow across the floor of Andrew's bedroom.

ANDREW: No—wait—don't leave me! I don't understand—what the hell is the point of all this? Why am I here? *Andrew walks toward the bedroom door as if he is going to follow Groves: then he stops.* Lydia! Lydia! What the hell is going on here?

* * *

Act II

The Ghost of
Conspiracy Theory Present

Andrew Dreams of Young Benjamin

It is now half past 1:00. Andrew has fallen asleep again. The master suite is in some disarray: the closet door is askew, half the blankets are on the floor, and the Californian's logbook is lying on Andrew's bureau, next to his cell phone.

Outside the French doors, the Washington Monument is again visible, its flood-lights muted and the blinking red lights at its pinnacle more prominent, fading in and out in the rhythm of a human heart.

As Andrew continues to sleep, the bedroom walls and the Monument fade away. The French doors transform into a small double-hung sash window, through which the rising sun begins to stream, illuminating a humble yellow kitchen, decorated with a battered pedestal table and three paint-spattered Windsor chairs. In the center of the table is a blue vase with a riot of perennial flowers trailing from it.

YOUNG BENJAMIN runs into the room, now flooded with the bright light of a mid-summer morning. He places a bathrobe on the end of Andrew's bed, stands and looks at his father for a minute, then runs lightly around the bed three times before climbing up on it. He grabs Andrew's feet and shakes them.

YOUNG BENJAMIN: Dad!

ANDREW: Mmmmmmmmm.

YOUNG BENJAMIN: Dad!

ANDREW: Mmmmm…mmmmmm.

YOUNG BENJAMIN: Come on Dad! Mom made coffee! You promised!

ANDREW: Ben…let me sleep…it's too early.

YOUNG BENJAMIN: Dad-dad–you promised!

ANDREW: Alright, alright.

A much younger ANDREW rises from the bed and puts on his bathrobe. The bed–with 50-something Andrew's dreaming body still in it-disappears into shadow.

YOUNG ANDREW walks to the pedestal table near the sash window, then moves to the window, yawning, and looks out.

YOUNG ANDREW: It's going to be a beautiful morning.

YOUNG BENJAMIN: I'll get my Lego, Dad!

YOUNG ANDREW: OK. And I'll get the coffee–how do you want yours?

YOUNG BENJAMIN: Dad–you know I don't like coffee!

YOUNG ANDREW: I know, I know.

Benjamin leaves the room. Andrew goes to the kitchen counter and pours himself a cup of coffee. He returns to the table and stands, looking out the window.

YOUNG ANDREW, *to himself:* Lydia's garden is really looking beautiful this summer.

Benjamin returns with his box of building bricks. He dumps them on the table and the pieces fly everywhere.

YOUNG ANDREW: Ben–that's a big mess.

YOUNG BENJAMIN: But we need a lot. To start.

Andrew sits down at the table.

YOUNG ANDREW: Do we? And why do we need a lot?

Benjamin starts picking up bricks off the floor and the chair and piling them on the table.

YOUNG BENJAMIN: Because we're going to build something Dad! I've got my black Lego, and my red Lego and my blue Lego, and my grey Lego, and my yellow Lego!

YOUNG ANDREW: Do you have any green Lego?

YOUNG BENJAMIN: Dad! You know I have some green Lego!

YOUNG ANDREW: OK, Ben. What are we going to build?

YOUNG BENJAMIN: I want to build a building, Dad. Something really special.

YOUNG ANDREW: OK, Ben–then you need a plan to start. And a vision.

Andrew starts to sort through the bricks, making stacks of colors and shapes.

YOUNG BENJAMIN: A vision?

YOUNG ANDREW: Yeah Ben, a vision. A way of thinking about what you want to build.

As they talk, Benjamin begins putting bricks together in very long rectangles. When he has enough, he starts to join them together.

YOUNG BENJAMIN: I want to build the biggest, greatest skyscraper in the world, Dad!

YOUNG ANDREW: OK. So...why do you want to build the biggest, greatest skyscraper in the world, Ben?

YOUNG BENJAMIN: Because I want to see how far it can go! I want to
live in the clouds!

YOUNG ANDREW: OK. So…you want to live in the clouds?

YOUNG BENJAMIN: Yeah, Dad–in the clouds...way way up high, in the
clouds.

YOUNG ANDREW: Why do you want to live in the clouds?

YOUNG BENJAMIN: I don't know. I just think it would be cool.

*Benjamin is putting bricks together in a very long block, but when he turns them
upright, they won't balance. His structure falls over.*

YOUNG BENJAMIN: Dad–it won't stand up, Dad.

YOUNG ANDREW: You're in too much of a hurry, Ben. If you want something to be strong, you have to take your time with it.

YOUNG BENJAMIN: Dad–

YOUNG ANDREW: Let me see, Ben. *Andrew starts to add a foundation to
the rectangles.* Hand me four of those long thin pieces.

YOUNG BENJAMIN: Here.

YOUNG ANDREW, *connecting the pieces:* See how that works? See how the
base is wider now?

YOUNG BENJAMIN, *leaning closer to watch:* Yeah–

YOUNG ANDREW: And see how each piece connects?

YOUNG BENJAMIN: Yeah–

YOUNG ANDREW: See–when they do that, then they are helping each
other–they hold each other in place. The whole building is stronger
that way.

YOUNG BENJAMIN: But shouldn't we fill in the spaces, Dad?

YOUNG ANDREW: Actually, no–this way, the building is more flexible. It can move a little.

YOUNG BENJAMIN: Move? Dad–buildings don't move.

YOUNG ANDREW: Actually, Ben–they do. Buildings move in all sorts of ways. They breathe. They adjust. They adapt. Just like we do.

YOUNG BENJAMIN, *stops playing for a moment and looks around the kitchen.* Does our house breathe?

YOUNG ANDREW: Yes it does, Ben.

YOUNG BENJAMIN: Is it alive?

YOUNG ANDREW: Well...buildings aren't alive in the way that people are. *Andrew pauses for a moment.* They don't have hearts and blood vessels and bones–

YOUNG BENJAMIN: Eeeew!

YOUNG ANDREW: But in their own way, in some ways, they are.

Andrew and Benjamin are quiet for a minute, building. The skyscraper is beginning to get very tall.

YOUNG BENJAMIN: Dad.

YOUNG ANDREW: Yes, Ben?

YOUNG BENJAMIN: Do you think we should move this to the floor?

YOUNG ANDREW: OK.

They move the skyscraper to the floor and continue working on it.

YOUNG BENJAMIN: Dad.

YOUNG ANDREW: Yes, Ben?

YOUNG BENJAMIN: Do you ever work on skyscrapers?

YOUNG ANDREW: No, Ben—I only work on ships. Navy ships.

YOUNG BENJAMIN: But did you always work on ships?

YOUNG ANDREW: No. I studied buildings in school. And I worked on buildings for a little while, afterwards. But then I started working on ships.

YOUNG BENJAMIN: Ships are strong, aren't they dad?

YOUNG ANDREW: Yes, Ben. Ships are very strong.

YOUNG BENJAMIN: And tall buildings are strong, right Dad?

YOUNG ANDREW: Yes, Ben. Tall buildings are very strong.

YOUNG BENJAMIN: What's the tallest building in the world, Dad? The Empire State Building?

YOUNG ANDREW: No Ben—not any more. The Twin Towers are the tallest buildings in the world now.

YOUNG BENJAMIN: The Twin Towers? There's two of them?

YOUNG ANDREW: Yeah. There's two of them.

YOUNG BENJAMIN: Wow. Two tallest buildings in the world.

Benjamin stops working on the skyscraper for moment. He stands up and pulls two of the Windsor chairs away from the table. He lines them up side by side, then resumes building.

YOUNG BENJAMIN: How tall are the Twin Towers, Dad?

YOUNG ANDREW: Oh, they're very tall...over one hundred stories, I think.

YOUNG BENJAMIN: Wow. Over one hundred stories. That's a lot of stories. How many stories do we have? *Benjamin starts to count the stories on their building.* One…two…three…four…

YOUNG ANDREW, *laughing:* I don't think we're quite there yet, Ben.

YOUNG BENJAMIN: How long did it take to build the Twin Towers, Dad?

YOUNG ANDREW: I can't say for sure, Ben—we'd have to look that up. But I do know that it takes time to make a building. Five, ten, even fifteen years, sometimes. Sometimes a lot longer.

YOUNG BENJAMIN: Ten years is a long time, Dad—that's longer than I've been alive!

YOUNG ANDREW: That's right.

YOUNG BENJAMIN: So am I like a building, Dad?

YOUNG ANDREW: Oh, you're way more complicated than any building.

Benjamin is adding pieces very quickly to their building—it starts to lean.

YOUNG ANDREW: Ben.

YOUNG BENJAMIN: What, Dad?

YOUNG ANDREW: See how fast you're trying to go?

YOUNG BENJAMIN: Yeah.

YOUNG ANDREW: Well, some things can't be hurried. Like how you had to learn to crawl before you walked?

YOUNG BENJAMIN: Yeah.

YOUNG ANDREW: If you build too fast, without thinking about what you're doing, you'll just slow yourself down.

YOUNG BENJAMIN: That's funny, Dad!

YOUNG ANDREW: It might be funny Ben, but it's also true. Sometimes you have to go slow to go fast.

YOUNG BENJAMIN: But Dad–that doesn't make any sense.

Andrew starts to add pieces to the bottom of the building, widening the base.

YOUNG ANDREW: Sure it does. You see, we can only build really tall buildings–we can only build at all–because we learned from what other people did before. And learning takes time–centuries, even. See what I just did?

Benjamin leans in to study the additional pieces around the bottom of the structure. Andrew lets go and the building sways, then stabilizes and stands on its own.

YOUNG BENJAMIN: Wow Dad! It stands up! *Benjamin takes a lap around the table.* So is that how they built the Twin Towers? They learned from someone else how to do it?

YOUNG ANDREW: Yes. In a way. You could say it that it took a thousand years to figure out how to build the Twin Towers.

YOUNG BENJAMIN: A thousand years! Wow Dad! *Benjamin starts to take another lap around the table—then stops suddenly.* But Dad...nobody lives that long.

YOUNG ANDREW: You're right Ben–individual people don't live that long. What I mean is it that it took all the knowledge and memories of a thousand years to get to the place where we could make those buildings.

YOUNG BENJAMIN: But Dad! How can we remember that long if we don't live for a thousand years?

YOUNG ANDREW, *laughing:* Well...we might not live that long, but some buildings–if they're really well designed–do live that long. Time is different when you're learning from buildings. Some of the things they did a thousand years ago are still there for us to look at, and think about.

Andrew and Benjamin resume their building task. They work in silence for a few minutes.

YOUNG BENJAMIN: Dad?

YOUNG ANDREW: Yes, Ben?

YOUNG BENJAMIN: Did you ever go inside them?

YOUNG ANDREW: Inside where?

YOUNG BENJAMIN: The Towers, Dad! The Twin Towers!

YOUNG ANDREW: No–I haven't been inside them.

YOUNG BENJAMIN: Well, I'm going to go inside them. And I'm going to ride all the way to the top! All the way way way up to the top. *Benjamin gets up from the floor, climbs up on the chairs, and then up on the table.* Dad?

YOUNG ANDREW: Yes, Ben?

YOUNG BENJAMIN, *starting to lose his balance:* I'm scared.

YOUNG ANDREW: Of what?

YOUNG BENJAMIN: Of the Twin Towers. Of going so high up.

Andrew picks up Benjamin and swings him back to the ground. They resume working on the skyscraper.

YOUNG ANDREW: Why are you scared of the Twin Towers, Ben?

YOUNG BENJAMIN: Well...maybe they could fall down.

YOUNG ANDREW: No, Benny–they can't fall down.

YOUNG BENJAMIN: Are you sure?

YOUNG ANDREW: Yes, Benny–I'm sure. They're very, very strong.

YOUNG BENJAMIN: How do they make them strong, Dad?

YOUNG ANDREW: Well, Ben–we make buildings strong in different ways.

YOUNG BENJAMIN: Like how, Dad?

YOUNG ANDREW: Well, sometimes, someone–like Michelangelo, for example–would make a building strong by using vaults.

YOUNG BENJAMIN: What's a vault?

YOUNG ANDREW: It's kind of like an arch–a series of arches. Arches are very strong. We've known about them for a long time.

YOUNG BENJAMIN: Do the Twin Towers use arches?

YOUNG ANDREW: No Ben–we know how to use materials differently now.

YOUNG BENJAMIN: What did they use to make the Twin Towers strong, Dad?

YOUNG ANDREW: They used concrete and steel.

Their building is starting to lean again. Benjamin touches it: it falls over, breaking into pieces.

YOUNG BENJAMIN: Dad! Now look what happened. It isn't strong enough! You said it would be strong enough.

YOUNG ANDREW: Actually, Ben, it's plenty strong—

YOUNG BENJAMIN: No, Dad–it isn't–

YOUNG ANDREW: The design is what's off.

YOUNG BENJAMIN: The design?

YOUNG ANDREW: Yeah. The way the building is put together…what makes it work.

Benjamin looks confused.

YOUNG ANDREW: Here—let me show you. *Andrew pulls a flower out of the vase in the center of the table.* Do you see this stem?

YOUNG BENJAMIN, *looking closely at it:* Yeah—

YOUNG ANDREW: What do you notice about it?

YOUNG BENJAMIN: It's hollow.

YOUNG ANDREW: That's right—if you bend it sideways, it will break, see?

Andrew starts to demonstrate.

YOUNG BENJAMIN: Mom's gonna get really mad if you bend her flower—

YOUNG ANDREW: Don't worry, we'll fix it. *Andrew bends the stem.* But see how it creases and starts to give way?

YOUNG BENJAMIN: Yeah—

Andrew flips the flower over so the stem is pointing up to the ceiling.

YOUNG ANDREW: But…if you push down on the stem—like this—feel that—

Benjamin pushes on the stem.

YOUNG ANDREW: What do you notice?

YOUNG BENJAMIN: It feels…strong.

YOUNG ANDREW: See…that's the structure…that's what's holding up the flower. In the middle of the stem it's hollow. All the strength is created by these channels on the outside. It's really strong. Each cell in the stem, in the circle, supports all the other cells in the circle. And the cells above and below make additional circles. They all hold each other up. The more something presses down from above, the stronger it is—that's what makes it stand up. *Andrew smiles playfully, teasing a bit.* See…that's a solid design.

YOUNG BENJAMIN: Is that the way the Towers are built?

YOUNG ANDREW: Yeah–that's the way the Towers are built. They're sort of like a hollow stem–a lot of the load–the way the buildings hold themselves up–is carried in these channels around the outside. And there are some in the middle too–which makes them even stronger.

YOUNG BENJAMIN: A stem inside a stem?

YOUNG ANDREW: Sort of.

YOUNG BENJAMIN: Wow.

YOUNG ANDREW: They're channels–columns–made of concrete and steel.

YOUNG BENJAMIN: Wow Dad! Flower stems made of concrete and steel!

Benjamin climbs onto the chairs again.

YOUNG BENJAMIN: So they could never fall down?

YOUNG ANDREW: Well–think of it this way, Ben. If you were a giant Godzilla monster–bigger than 100 stories tall– and you were very very very strong...

YOUNG BENJAMIN, *jumping off the chairs:* Rroah!!!!!

YOUNG ANDREW: ...and you went up and pushed one of the Towers over– sideways–if you pushed it very very very hard–you could break a piece of it off–

He demonstrates with their building.

YOUNG BENJAMIN: Just like the stem on Mom's flower?

YOUNG ANDREW: Just like the stem on Mom's flower. You can bend the stem, or break a piece of it off, but the flower would never fall down in a big pile.

YOUNG BENJAMIN: No. Flowers just wilt. Like the time you forgot to water Mom's flower garden.

YOUNG ANDREW: Yeah. Like the time I forgot to water Mom's garden.

YOUNG BENJAMIN, *studying the flower closely:* An engineer did that? Made the Twin Towers like a flower stem?

YOUNG ANDREW: An architect did. An architect had the vision. The engineers figured out how to build the Towers…how to make them safe.

YOUNG BENJAMIN: They're safe because of engineers…engineers like you, Dad.

YOUNG ANDREW: That's right. They're safe because of engineers.

YOUNG BENJAMIN: And the engineers built them?

YOUNG ANDREW: A lot of people built them, Benny. Buildings aren't made by one person. There's not only an architect, and an engineer–actually, there are sometimes lots of architects, and there are the people who make the architect's drawings–that's called drafting–and there are lots of different kinds of engineers–who do different jobs–and then there are the tradespeople. Welders, electricians, pipefitters, riveters, tile setters…lots and lots of people, doing different jobs. And then there are the people who bring the materials to the site–and the people who make those materials…the glass for the windows, the fiber for the carpets, the porcelain for the sinks and toilets–

YOUNG BENJAMIN, *running in circles around the table:* The toilets! People who make the toilets!

YOUNG ANDREW: Yes, Benny...and the people who take things off the site...they count too. And the building inspectors, and the people who write the safety codes...

Andrew pauses, watching Benjamin circle the table.

YOUNG ANDREW: It's like a big dance. No one builds alone. We build together.

Benjamin climbs onto the chairs again, and stands with one foot on each chair.

YOUNG BENJAMIN: Is an architect the boss, Dad? I want to be the boss!

YOUNG ANDREW: No, Benny—not really. Architects and engineers and tradespeople-we all work together. Architects come up with the vision. Engineers come up with the plan for how to do it. Tradespeople make it happen. Everyone has a part. It's a collaboration.

YOUNG BENJAMIN: A collaboration?

YOUNG ANDREW: Yeah. Teamwork.

YOUNG BENJAMIN: Teamwork.

Andrew picks Benjamin up, swings him around, and sets him down on the chairs again.

YOUNG ANDREW: So whenever you see a building—especially a really beautiful building, old or new, remember that people made that together.

YOUNG BENJAMIN: Just like us—today!

YOUNG ANDREW: Just like us, today.

YOUNG BENJAMIN: And I'm the architect: I'm the one with the vision!

YOUNG ANDREW: That's right, Ben. You're the one with the vision.

YOUNG BENJAMIN: And you're the engineer: you're the one that makes it safe.

YOUNG ANDREW: That's right Ben. I'm the engineer. I'm the one that makes it safe.

The kitchen, with Young Andrew and Young Benjamin still working on their building, fades away. In the dark, Young Benjamin speaks one last time, his voice distant and echoing—as if he is in a long, narrow tunnel.

YOUNG BENJAMIN: Someday, Dad, I'm going to work in the tallest building in the world. And when I do, I'm not going to worry...because I know...that the engineers made it safe.

From the shadows, Andrew's bed—with 50-something Andrew still sleeping soundly in it—reappears. The moonlight intensifies and the walls and French doors of the bedroom suite become visible again: outside, the Washington Monument is now shrouded in deep purple shadow.

On the bureau, Andrew's cell phone lights up. After a moment, it begins to ring. The ringing grows louder and louder, then the phone switches to voicemail.

Andrew's bedroom is filled with the sound of 20-something Benjamin's voice speaking from the phone.

BENJAMIN: Dad—Dad—it's me—Ben. Listen—something just happened, over at Tower One—I'm not sure what—but—I just wanted to remind you—I'm not in Tower One—I'm in Tower Two—and I'm OK. Call me when you get this. I love you.

Andrew bolts up in bed, chest heaving. Through the French doors, the Washington Monument is now awash in red light.

Andrew stares at the Monument, then doubles over and covers his face with his hands.

ANDREW: Ben. Ben. Ben.

* * *

John F Kennedy Visits

It is now 2 a.m. Andrew rises from his bed and goes to the bureau. He picks up his cell phone, checks to make sure it is turned off, and walks into the main loft area—where he stops, stunned by what he sees.

Arrayed around his dining table are the artifacts of a meeting that has been interrupted: notebooks, pens and pencils, coffee cups, half eaten pastries. Along the far wall of his penthouse, the trio of French doors and the view of the Washington Monument has disappeared. Instead, a group of people in office attire are standing along a series of tall, narrow windows, looking outside.

The light coming in through the windows is that of a bright, early September morning—but there is a flickering, smoky cast to the light.

As Andrew stands looking at the people and taking in the changes to his loft, the elevator chimes. Its doors glide open, and three more people step out. The elevator closes silently behind them. They pass Andrew as if he is invisible.

OFFICE WORKER ONE, *rushing toward the people at the window:* We heard something in the elevator!

OFFICE WORKER TWO, *dropping a briefcase beside the table:* Yeah—the whole thing shook—what happened?

Andrew begins to approach the wall of windows, then stops. Instead, he walks to the table, pushes aside a notebook, and sets his cell phone down.

The office workers at the windows do not appear to notice Andrew. Instead, they speak in murmurs to each other, and continually turn back toward the windows. Then, one of them grimaces and turns away, a look of horror on her face. The others step back, visibly stunned by something that is happening outside.

The light streaming in through the windows intensifies, becoming tinged with red. The elevator chimes again, and the people freeze in stop action, then disappear into shadow. The elevator doors open, and JOHN F. KENNEDY steps out.

JFK: Ah, Mr. Blossom–good–you're already here. *He walks to the credenza where Andrew keeps his scotch and pours himself a double.* Ice?

ANDREW: Uh–it's underneath–on the left.

JFK finds the ice, drops a few cubes into his glass. He takes a slow drink, clearly enjoying it–then gestures toward the credenza.

JFK: Very nice–Brazilian cherry, isn't it?

ANDREW, *visibly distracted—he keeps turning toward the windows and the people shrouded in shadow:* What?

JFK: Never mind them, Mr. Blossom.

ANDREW: What?

JFK: The people standing by the windows. We'll get to them–but first, we have some other business to attend to.

ANDREW: Other business?

JFK: Yes.

ANDREW: And what business would that be?

JFK, *mildly surprised:* Weren't you briefed?

ANDREW: I have no idea what you are talking about.

At the windows, the light dims, then intensifies again: JFK and Andrew both turn toward the windows for a moment, then look back at each other.

ANDREW: What the hell is going on here?

JFK: I don't have a lot of time, Mr. Blossom. Let's get started.

ANDREW: Get started with what?

JFK: It's time to show up, Mr. Blossom.

JFK pours two more drinks.

ANDREW: Show up?

JFK walks to Andrew and hands him a drink.

JFK: Show up. It's a leadership concept–that positive change occurs when people choose to show up.

ANDREW: What the hell is that supposed to mean?

Andrew tosses back his drink. JFK follows suit, then takes the glass from Andrew and walks to the table. He sets both glasses down.

JFK: Do you know where you are right now, Mr. Blossom?

ANDREW, *adamant:* My penthouse. I'm in my penthouse. And I have no idea why you are here. *He gestures toward the office workers.* Or why they're here.

JFK: It already happened Mr. Blossom. Denying it won't make it go away.

ANDREW: What are you talking about?

JFK: Where are you right now?

ANDREW: I'm in my penthouse!

JFK: Look again.

ANDREW: Penthouse.

JFK: Mr. Blossom—

ANDREW: PENTHOUSE!

Andrew's phone starts to ring; Andrew freezes, staring at it. The phone continues to ring.

JFK: Are you going to answer that?

ANDREW: No.

JFK: Why not?

ANDREW: Because I–I–I turned it off. *To himself:* I'm sure of it.

JFK crosses to the table, picks up the phone, and answers it.

JFK: Jack here. *He listens, then hands the phone to Andrew.* It's your wife.

ANDREW: Hello? *Listening:* Yes. Yes. Yes. I understand. I will.

Andrew hangs up the phone and places it back on the table. Then he picks it up again, and fumbles with it until he has assured himself that it is really turned off. Only then does he respond to JFK.

ANDREW: All right. I'll try.

JFK: Very good then. May we begin?

ANDREW: Sure. Whatever.

JFK: Mr. Blossom.

ANDREW: Yes?

JFK: Where are you right now?

ANDREW, *whispering:* I'm–in the Tower. Tower Two. The South Tower.

JFK: And what do you see, Mr. Blossom?

ANDREW: I-I-see people looking out–they're looking out the windows. *He starts to pace.* Jesus–I can't deal with this–

JFK: Yes, you can, Mr. Blossom.

ANDREW: No, I can't–can't we just move on, get it over with???

JFK: What are we supposed to move on to, Mr. Blossom? *He gestures toward the room and the office workers, still shrouded in shadow.* This already happened. The task now is to look clearly at it, to try to understand–

Andrew's face reddens. His pacing becomes more constrained as he tries to avoid looking at the office workers while staying as far away as he can from JFK and the table.

ANDREW: What's to understand? Some terrorists hit our buildings with planes. The buildings collapsed. We punished them, and we've gone on. End of story.

JFK: Is it.

ANDREW: Is it what?

JFK: The end of the story.

ANDREW, *stops pacing:* Of course it is! We took care of that! We've moved on.

JFK: You've moved on?

ANDREW: What?

JFK: You've moved on? *He gazes firmly at Andrew.* Because you don't seem to have moved on at all, Mr. Blossom.

ANDREW, *avoiding eye contact:* I have no idea what you are talking about.

JFK: You've alienated your sister–

ANDREW: My sister is naturally alienated–

JFK: You've destroyed most of your business relationships–

ANDREW: My business relationships are just fine!

JFK: You drink far too much–

ANDREW: Everybody in DC drinks too much–

JFK: And tell me again why you didn't want to answer that phone?

ANDREW: I–I–didn't–I didn't...say.

JFK: That's right. You didn't say.

ANDREW: And I don't have to.

JFK: No. You don't. You can continue doing exactly what you're doing–but this–and the aftermath of this—*he gestures to the windows and people*–isn't going to go away because you refuse to look directly at it ...any more than the crew of the Californian could erase what they witnessed in the North Atlantic the night the Titanic sank. *He directs another steady gaze at Andrew.* History exerts an influence, Mr. Blossom, even when we send things down the memory hole.

ANDREW, *vaguely confused...as if struggling to remember something important:* The memory hole.

JFK: The memory hole, Mr. Blossom–the place we put things when we don't want to deal with them. With their implications.

ANDREW: What are you–some kind of conspiracy theorist?

JFK remains silent.

ANDREW, *embarrassed:* Look. I'm sorry. I just don't understand what's going on here. Lydia asked me to listen to–to you–but, well, I don't get it. The Titanic, the Twin Towers, the memory hole. I mean, if that's what you're doing, if you're pushing some kind of–of–of tinfoil hat conspiracy from beyond the grave–if that's what you're getting at–I'm sorry–Lydia, I'm sorry, I love you but–well, just forget it–you're wasting your time, because I'm not buying–

Andrew begins to pace again–this time more rapidly. He seems to have lost track of his surroundings.

ANDREW, *to himself:* I mean, really–the Apollo moon landings didn't happen, Jesus was Illuminati, what the hell, what is wrong with these people?

JFK, *softly:* What is wrong with *what* people, Mr. Blossom?

Andrew startles. He appears confused–as if the question has brought him back from some other place in his mind.

ANDREW: What?

JFK: What is wrong with <u>what</u> people?

ANDREW: People who...people who are always looking for reasons to doubt–

JFK: Doubt what, Mr. Blossom?

ANDREW: What kind of a question is that? Doubt the things that happen, of course!

JFK: And how do people figure that out?

ANDREW: Figure what out?

JFK: In a given situation, what happened.

ANDREW: I have no idea what you're talking about. *He starts to pace again.* And even if you are trying to make some kind of valid connection–hell–I don't get that either. The Titanic hit an iceberg–it was an accident. This—*Andrew gestures toward the people at the window*—this was no damn accident. The people who did this–they—they–needed to–

As Andrew talks, JFK returns to the credenza, pours another scotch, walks to Andrew and hands it to him.

JFK: Go ahead, Mr. Blossom.

Andrew throws back the drink, then stands with the empty glass in his hand, as if he is unsure what to do with it. JFK watches him very intently, saying nothing for a time, then reaches out and takes the glass.

JFK: Mr. Blossom.

ANDREW: Yes?

JFK: I'm curious about something.

JFK sets the glass down on the table.

ANDREW: What?

JFK: Do you consider yourself a patriot?

ANDREW: What?

JFK: A patriot. Do you consider yourself one.

ANDREW: I–I–of course I do.

JFK: And what does that word mean to you?

ANDREW: What?

JFK: Patriot. What does that word mean to you?

ANDREW: I expect it means what it's always meant—

JFK: Which is what, exactly?

The phone starts to ring again. Andrew freezes, watching it ring. On the third ring, Andrew rushes to the table, grabs the phone and fumbles with it, trying to turn off the ringer.

JFK: Mr. Blossom.

Andrew silences the phone: he places it back on the table.

ANDREW, *irritated:* Yes?

JFK: What do you think your son would say about the concept of being a patriot–if he were here?

ANDREW, *half whispering/half snarling:* I'm not talking about my son. Do not bring up my son.

JFK responds with silence.

ANDREW: My son is dead. He's dead.

JFK: Yes, I know. *He pauses.* So is mine.

ANDREW: You didn't bury yours.

JFK: No. He buried me.

There is a long pause as Andrew and JFK study each other.

ANDREW: I'm sorry...for your loss...your losses.

JFK: And I, for yours.

Another long pause. For a moment, the people at the windows appear to be moving, then they freeze into another shadowy tableau. JFK notes the movement at the windows and glances at his wristwatch.

JFK: Mr. Blossom–I know this is difficult. But it's important. You've already made every obvious move on the board. So let's try again–please. What do you think your son would say–about the concept of patriotism–if he were here right now?

ANDREW, *looking around, as if he has just realized where he is:* Ben. Ben! Is he here? Can I see him???? Can I talk to him?

JFK, *softly:* Mr. Blossom–he isn't here.

ANDREW: He is–he could be–the–this–this is the South Tower, isn't it?

JFK: Mr. Blossom.

ANDREW, *starting to pace again:* It hasn't happened yet–it hasn't been hit yet, Ben, he could still be alive–

JFK: Mr. Blossom–please try to focus–

ANDREW, *covering his face with his hands:* NO!! NO!

JFK: What would Ben say?

ANDREW, *whispering:* I can't say. I don't know. *There is a long pause, then Andrew speaks in a whisper, without removing his hands from his face.* What would **your** son say?

JFK: I'm sorry?

ANDREW, *whispering slightly louder:* What would your son say?

JFK: John? Hmm. Fair question. *JFK studies the windows and the shadowy tableau.* You know–I died when John was still very young. I didn't have the time with him that you had with Ben...but...I'd like to think that he inherited the courage of the family line–as well as some of his mother's resolve.

ANDREW, *still whispering:* And?

JFK: And if he were here...well, I'd like to think that he would say...let's look at it. Let's try to look at what's happened–without wrapping ourselves in a flag...a flag that–and I think he might say this as well, though I'm sorry to admit it–a flag that doesn't have the same meaning, anymore.

ANDREW, *dropping his hands from his face–which is now blood red—and shouting:* What? Who says that! How can you say that? Maybe it doesn't have the same meaning to you–but it has–it matters–it has meaning for some people!

JFK responds with silence.

ANDREW, *quietly:* It has meaning for me.

JFK continues to stare evenly at Andrew, saying nothing.

ANDREW: I'm sorry. It's just that–well, things have changed. They've changed.

The elevator chimes, softly. JFK looks at his wristwatch again, then back at Andrew.

JFK: Mr. Blossom–what do you know about lifeboats?

ANDREW: Lifeboats?

JFK: Yes–lifeboats. You're an engineer, aren't you? You spent most of your career in naval engineering, didn't you? This world you're a part of now–defense contracting–it isn't what you really know, is it? *He pauses for a moment, then continues:* Tell me about lifeboats.

ANDREW: We're in Tower Two and you want to talk about lifeboats?

JFK says nothing.

ANDREW: All right, all right. What about them?

JFK: What's the function of a lifeboat, Mr. Blossom?

ANDREW: Uh...well...it's–it's part of a calculated risk management strategy.

JFK: Which means what?

ANDREW: Which means...you hope you won't need one...but if you do, you want it to be there.

JFK: Which means what?

ANDREW: Uh...someone has to think about it ahead of time–supplies, passive or active, launch capabilities...a lot of detail work. It's highly specialized.

JFK: You don't leave it out, then...isn't that right? You don't leave it to chance.

ANDREW: That's right. Nothing–if possible–left to chance.

JFK: And the last thing you want–in the event of a disaster–is a panicked rush to the lifeboats. Isn't that correct?

ANDREW: That's right...you don't want to rush the lifeboats. It will just make a bad situation worse.

JFK: Plan your work, work your plan. That sort of thing. Chance favors the prepared mind. Is that it?

ANDREW: I suppose so. Look–Mr. Pres–Mr. Kennedy–

JFK: Please–call me Jack.

ANDREW: What? Look–Ja–Mr. Pres–I-I-I don't understand. Where are you going with this?

JFK: Stay with me, Mr. Blossom. Let's assume a scenario where an accident–an incident–of some sort has occurred.

ANDREW: On the ocean?

JFK: Right. Maybe. Don't be so literal–just go with it for the moment, OK?

ANDREW: OK.

JFK: Imagine an accident, and imagine some lifeboats...evidence that somewhere, somehow, some planning has been done...where people can see, however dimly, that they have options–not ideal maybe, not a lot of options, but there are choices. Someone has thought to build and provide a lifeboat.

ANDREW: OK.

JFK: In such a situation, what do you think could explain the phenomena of people choosing not to get in?

ANDREW: What are you talking about?

JFK: Let's take the Titanic, Mr. Blossom. Think about it. Why were so many lifeboats empty?

ANDREW: How should I know!

JFK: Think about it.

ANDREW: I suppose some people were afraid to get in.

JFK: That's possible.

ANDREW: And some people didn't understand how serious the situation was.

JFK: Also possible.

ANDREW: And some people didn't have the opportunity–the people below decks.

JFK: All right. Those are all very plausible explanations.

ANDREW: And your point?

JFK: Is it also possible, Mr. Blossom, that some of the people on the Titanic saw the lights of the Californian out on the horizon?

ANDREW: I...suppose so.

JFK: And is it possible that in the calculus of their minds, it was better to wait for those lights to come closer–to wait for someone else to rescue them, than to act on the situation in the moment? To continue on, business as usual, to passively wait, rather than to think through the potential consequences of staying where they were?

ANDREW: I–I suppose so.

JFK: And in failing to think–and in failing to act decisively, is it possible their fate was sealed?

ANDREW: I don't know. Maybe. What's your point?

JFK: My point is that sometimes survival depends upon doing something that–in the moment–appears counter-intuitive.

ANDREW: Counter-intuitive?

JFK: Yes. The dial is spinning, you can't get a read–and what you think you should do is exactly the wrong thing. The maladaptive thing.

ANDREW: Maladaptive?

JFK: A mistake.

ANDREW: So...Lydia sent you here to tell me I've made a mistake. What mistake? I'm a good man. I work hard. I'm honest. What mistake could I possibly have made?

JFK: Imagine yourself on the Titanic, Mr. Blossom. Something's happened—you're not sure what, but you think it's bad—the crew—the experts, those in the know—they look pretty worried. And yet...you can see lights on the horizon. Someone is out there.

ANDREW: OK...

JFK: And then a crew member tells you that you should get in this tiny wooden boat, and descend 150+ feet into the dark of the cold North Atlantic—but you can see that there's a ship out there. Would you do it?

ANDREW: What does this have to do with me?

JFK: Would you get in the lifeboat, or stay where you are? Cold North Atlantic, or this solid-feeling ship, with the lights still on, and maybe even a cup of tea waiting in the cabin. *JFK pauses.* Would you get in the lifeboat? Or stay where you are?

ANDREW: I am completely lost.

JFK: I know. You've been lost for a long time. *JFK pauses again, studying Andrew.* Let's try another tack. Look around you again. Where are we?

ANDREW: We're in the Tower. Tower Two.

JFK: That's right. The South Tower. On the 86th floor. And Tower One—the North Tower—has just been been hit.

ANDREW: I know.

JFK: How much time do they have, Mr. Blossom?

ANDREW: Oh no. No no no no. I see where you're going now...

JFK: No, you don't. *JFK pauses.* How much time do they have, Mr. Blossom? In Tower Two?

ANDREW: No.

JFK: Do you know?

ANDREW: Of course I know.

JFK: How much time?

ANDREW: Please.

JFK: Mr. Blossom.

ANDREW, *whispering:* Please.

JFK: Mr. Blossom. How much time?

ANDREW, *whispering:* Sixteen minutes.

JFK, *softly:* That's right. Sixteen minutes, more or less. *JFK gestures toward the people standing at the window.* Sixteen minutes. To act. To decide whether to make a move. The people on the Titanic...at least, those who had the option–they had a little more time...around two hours and twenty minutes, if I recall.

ANDREW: I still don't get the connection.

JFK: You've had a little more time.

ANDREW: What?

JFK: You've had a little more time.

ANDREW: I wasn't on the Titanic. And I wasn't here when this happened.

JFK: I know. *JFK pauses again, then speaks very carefully.* But what if Ben's 911 was your iceberg?

ANDREW: What if Ben's 911 was my iceberg? What?

JFK: That's right—what if Ben's 911 was your iceberg? What if, all this time—the last 14 years—the clock's been ticking, and your chance to get in a lifeboat has been slipping away?

ANDREW: What lifeboat? Why do I need a lifeboat?

JFK: You said it yourself, Mr. Blossom—it's a risk management strategy. The nature of any disaster is that, at a certain point, the circumstances of the future, which make themselves known first in the moment of a critical event—the ship hits the iceberg, the plane hits the tower—overwhelm the business of the present. Even for the most agile people—like Ben. *JFK pauses. Both men look at the people near the window, still shrouded in shadow.* It's in the time between the first indicator and its follow-on effects that you have to act—to even have a chance at survival.

ANDREW: Ben was not overwhelmed. Ben was murdered.

The elevator chimes again—this time louder.

JFK: Mr. Blossom. You—like the crew of the Californian—were a witness to a tragedy. A tragedy. But you're also caught in a larger critical event—one of planetary proportions. And from what I can tell, you haven't given much thought to your lifeboat.

ANDREW: You really are off the hook.

JFK: Your wife said you'd be resistant—I believe her words were dense as pig iron—but your density is an easy out at this point, Mr. Blossom, and it won't save you. And it won't save any of the people you care about...that is, if you still care about anyone at all.

ANDREW: Of course I care. Of course I do.

JFK: Then mark my words, Mr. Blossom: this event already happened...but its significance has yet to be perceived. And because of that, you—like the passengers on the Titanic—are working from a very faulty map.

ANDREW: I really have no fucking idea what you are talking about.

JFK: These situations are scattered like jewels at your feet, Mr. Blossom. But instead of picking them up and studying them, you've let yourself be distracted by the instant replay, and the search for the smoking gun.

ANDREW: It's not that easy to get rid of the replay.

JFK: No, it isn't–especially if you're always running from what's underneath. Denial really jams up the radar.

ANDREW: What are you talking about?

JFK: I think you know.

ANDREW: No, I assure you...I don't.

JFK: Ask yourself why you never heard of the Californian.

ANDREW: How should I know?

JFK: OK. Then how about this–why does the lone nut theory in Dallas–my personal favorite–continually renew itself?

ANDREW: I have no idea. Never paid it any mind.

JFK: Fair enough. Then how about this one: why do you–a structural engineer–choose to believe that your son died in the collapse of a building that you know perfectly well could not have been destroyed in the manner portrayed?

ANDREW: I will not answer that.

JFK: Where do unresolved things go, when we try to forget about them, Mr. Blossom?

Andrew's phone rings again. Andrew startles, then freezes.

ANDREW, *looking with horror toward the phone:* No.

JFK: Are you going to answer that, Mr. Blossom?

ANDREW: No.

JFK: Why not?

ANDREW: No-I–

JFK: Why not?

ANDREW: Because I–

JFK: Because you what?

ANDREW: Because I–I–

JFK: Yes?

ANDREW: Because I–I turned it off, it's supposed to be off, it's not supposed to be ringing–

Andrew's phone goes to voicemail.

BENJAMIN, *from the phone:* Dad–Dad–it's me–Ben. Listen–something just happened, over at Tower One–I'm not sure what–but–I just wanted to remind you–I'm not in Tower One–I'm in Tower Two–and I'm—

ANDREW: NO!!!!!!!

Andrew rushes to the table, grabs his cellphone and hurls it against the wall. As it shatters, the people near the windows begin to move again: the light outside intensifies, casting yellow red shadows into the room.

JFK: Why won't you answer the phone, Mr. Blossom?

ANDREW, *pacing again:* Because I can't–

JFK: Why not?

ANDREW: Because I can't!

JFK: Why not?

ANDREW, *pacing more rapidly, as if he is trapped in a small cage and is trying to find a way out:* Lydia! Why are you doing this to me???

JFK: Why not, Mr. Blossom?

ANDREW: Because!

JFK: Because why?

ANDREW: Because I-

JFK: Yes?

ANDREW: Because I–I didn't.

JFK: You didn't what?

ANDREW: Because I didn't answer—

JFK: You didn't answer what?

ANDREW: It–I didn't answer IT!

JFK: IT?

Andrew stops pacing and stands rooted in one place, screaming.

ANDREW: IT! IT! The phone! The god-damned phone! The phone rang, and it was him, it was Ben–he called me–

The elevator chimes rapidly and loudly. The doors open and close repeatedly and appear to be vibrating. The elevator floor jerks erratically, as if it is about to fall. Faintly, the sound of jet engines can be heard.

ANDREW, *anguished and furious:* He called me that morning, from, from here. Lydia was out of town...and I had the radio off...and I was too god-damned busy–and I didn't...I didn't...I let it go...I let it go...I let it go to voicemail–and I –Oh,

Andrew staggers toward the wall, striking it with his shoulder. He crumples into a ball on the floor.

ANDREW: Ben–Ben. I'm sorry I'm sorry I'm so so so sorry.

JFK: Mr. Blossom. *JFK waits for Andrew to respond.*

ANDREW, *curled up and sobbing-oblivious to the scene around him:* I lost my son–my son–

JFK: Mr. Blossom. Anything you do now–of value–

ANDREW: No-no-

JFK: Mr. Blossom–

ANDREW: No...my son–Ben...

JFK: That's your truth, Mr. Blossom–that's your North Star. That's the only thing strong enough to unjam the radar.

ANDREW: No. Nothing is true anymore–nothing–

JFK: No–you're confusing ideas with experiences, Mr. Blossom. You still have truth–

ANDREW: I don't–

JFK: You do.

ANDREW: I can't–

JFK: You can. If you choose to.

JFK approaches Andrew–who is still curled up on the floor–and crouches down next to him.

JFK: You know, Mr. Blossom–the crew on the Californian–they had no idea what they were looking at–but at least they tried, later, as a group, to figure it out. *He pauses.* But you–you're, well...different. You've chosen–actively–not just to ignore the real impact of that day ...to deny it. And to insist others deny it as well.

ANDREW: I'm not ignoring anything! I'm not denying anything! It's just too fucking complicated: I can't make sense of it! Nobody can make sense of it!

JFK: Mr. Blossom...It's not your job to make sense of it. Meaning making is an edifice, every bit as complex as a building–it's a collective endeavor. If you had a dozen lifetimes, you couldn't do it on your own. *JFK stands and walks toward the elevator. As the doors glide open to receive him, he turns back to Andrew.* And at the moment of a critical incident, retrospective analysis is beside the point. After the iceberg hits, the goal is to get in the lifeboat.

With great effort, Andrew struggles to his feet. He stumbles forward toward the table, and braces himself against it.

ANDREW: What lifeboats? Whose lifeboats? Why do I need a lifeboat?

JFK steps inside the elevator: its doors and floor are quivering now, as if the building's structure is resisting some tremendous, invisible force. The sound of jet engines is growing louder.

JFK: I think you know the answer to that question.

ANDREW: What? No! No I don't! Whose lifeboat? What are you talking about? What am I supposed to do now? No–please wait!

JFK: Good day, Mr. Blossom.

The elevator doors close. As they do, an explosion takes place. The conference room—and the people at the windows—disappears in a flash of light. Andrew crouches behind the table, covering his ears.

ANDREW: No. No. No.

Explosive debris fills the air: as the noise dissipates and the debris settles, the World Trade Center Plaza—and the main lobby entrance to World Trade Center 1—becomes visible.

Sirens sound in the distance. Emergency lights flash. From multiple directions, first responders appear, carrying gear, speaking on radios, dodging one another and the shards of glass and metal still falling from above.

A trio of firefighters weave their way through the chaos: they stop in front of the lobby entrance. One of them is holding a radio, from which static and coded discussions emanate.

The firefighter radios for instructions: as they wait for a reply, the firefighters look up toward the top of WTC1.

FIREFIGHTER ONE: What the hell?

FIREFIGHTER TWO: They're jumping.

FIREFIGHTER ONE: They're jumping?

FIREFIGHTER TWO: Yeah—they're jumping. Don't look. Don't—

The third firefighter—who is very young—watches the trajectory of a fall: he visibly and strongly reacts as it strikes the ground. The others witness his response.

FIREFIGHTER ONE: Don't look, Sammy. Don't look.

FIREFIGHTER TWO: Come on—let's go—we've got to get up there.

The firefighters disappear into the chaos; more people appear; city administrators in suits, security guards, office workers. A pair of news reporters stops and sets up their camera.

NEWSCASTER: Take one. Take one and two. One. This is as close as we can get to the base of the World Trade Center. As you can see, here at the Towers, the debris continues to fall and to rain on the people below...people are hanging from the windows 90 stories up...and a number of bodies have actually hit the pavement.

CAMERA OPERATOR: Should we do another one?

NEWSCASTER: Take two. Take two and two. One. This is as close as we can get to the base of the World Trade Centers. You can see the firemen assembled here, police officers, FBI agents, the Towers...a huge explosion now raining debris on all of us–

A rush of air engulfs the newscasters and other people milling about, and is followed by rhythmic explosions and the rippling sound of a wall of falling debris. The sound lasts for 11 seconds; Andrew is crouched behind his dining room table, his hands over his ears.

ANDREW: No. No. No.

FDNY BATTALION CHIEF, *voice over:* Tower Two is down. Evacuate Tower One.

Sirens. Flashing lights. People pass in shadows now. There is much less talk on the radios. Then the rush of air, the explosions, and the debris cascade repeats, this time 9.5 seconds in duration. In its wake, a thick cloud of white dust obscures everything.

Silence descends. Through the dust, emergency lights dimly flash. People again begin to pass by, walking quickly, heads down, holding their jackets and shirts to their faces.

The three firefighters emerge again, covered in dust.

FIREFIGHTER ONE, *speaking into his radio:* We're in Tower Two.

DISPATCHER, *from firefighter's radio:* Where are you?

FIREFIGHTER ONE: Tower Two.

FIREFIGHTER TWO, *looking around:* Where is Tower Two?

DISPATCHER: Where are you?

FIREFIGHTER ONE: I said we're in Tower Two.

Light begins streaming through the dust. The firefighters stand, dumbstruck, as the light reveals that the buildings are completely gone. Andrew is sitting up, and is looking at them, his pajama top up over his nose and mouth.

FIREFIGHTER ONE: Where is Tower Two?

Out of the dust, sunlight behind them, four string players, dripping wet and carrying their instruments, emerge. They stand together in a loose circle alongside the firefighters, looking at the scene and at each other.

The sound of a circuit breaker being thrown is heard: as if struck, Andrew falls backward, unconscious.

* * *

Act III

The Ghost of
Conspiracy Theory Future

Falling Man Visits

It is now 3 a.m. Andrew is lying unconscious on the floor of the main loft area. On the table are remnants of the office workers' meeting. JFK's scotch glass is on the credenza. On the floor near Andrew lie tattered pieces of the Californian's log book. There is a large dark patch on the wall, as if it has been scorched.

The interior of the penthouse is shrouded in dark blue light. Outside the French doors, the moon has disappeared, and the Washington Monument no longer casts a shadow. The red lights at its pinnacle are dim and flickering—barely visible— and the Monument appears flat and 2-dimensional.

The elevator chimes softly and its doors glide quietly open. FALLING MAN steps out. He is dressed in traditional wait-staff attire: black trousers, black tennis shoes, and a white button-down shirt. His shirt is partially untucked: underneath, he is wearing an orange t-shirt.

Falling Man picks up a dining chair lying on its side next to the elevator. He carries it to the table: using it like a stair, he climbs onto the table top. Picking his way through the pens and notebooks, Falling Man finds a comfortable place to stand, then raises his hands slightly above his hips, as if preparing for a dive. In a subtle motion, he sweeps his hands downward: as he does, the rich, broken, opening chords of Bach's Chaconne (from the Partita No. 2 in D Minor) fill the room.

As the resonant sounds of the Chaconne fill the air, Falling Man begins to or- chestrate the speed and volume of the music and the motion of stars in the night sky, which he has illuminated within Andrew's penthouse. This capacity seems to fascinate and delight Falling Man, as if he is revisiting an ability he has forgotten he possesses.

Andrew stirs, wakes, and sits up. He sees Falling Man.

ANDREW, *very softly, with deep exhaustion and resignation in his voice*: You must be another of Lydia's friends.

Falling Man nods to Andrew as he continues to play with the stars and the music. Andrew nods in reply, then he lies back down, mesmerized by the stars wheeling overhead.

A minute passes: then Falling Man jumps lightly from the table to the chair and from the chair to the ground. He reaches out to help Andrew stand up. Andrew takes Falling Man's hand and stands–clearly dizzy. Using the back of the chair, Andrew braces himself.

Falling Man steps away: again, he uses his body and the music to shape and change the light. Night fades away, along with the walls of Andrew's penthouse and the view of the Washington Monument, leaving Andrew, his chair, and Falling Man surrounded by a bleak, empty darkness.

Falling Man continues to move, magician–like, through the darkness: as he does, the sky again fills with stars, which wheel slowly overhead, followed by a rising sun and a blue sky filled with scudding cumulous clouds.

Falling Man continues to play with the light, and the days and nights appear to pass faster and faster, as if the earth's rotation has been sped up. The shadows grow long, then short, in concert with the passing and changing of the seasons.

ANDREW: Where are we going, Spirit?

Falling Man gestures, and he and Andrew are standing in a courtyard: beyond low–set stucco walls, the rolling hills of a vineyard are visible.

Inside the courtyard stands an ancient tree, its thick branches reaching out in all directions. The autumn sun is beginning to set behind the tree: golden streams of light sparkle off the vibrant reds and oranges of its leaves. Beneath the tree is Andrew's dining table, now in its natural habitat.

Falling Man creates a wind and mixes it with the music: as he does, a group of 30-something adults enter the courtyard from all directions, bringing with them strings of solar lights, a white table cloth, plates of food, a case of wine and beer, a large, flower-covered wedding cake, and a guitar.

As the party finishes decorating the courtyard, a preacher enters, followed by a tall young man with curly dark hair and a trim beard, and a young woman, who is clearly pregnant: she is wearing an antique wedding dress.

ANDREW: Oh! It's Leah! Leah and Paul!

Falling Man continues to orchestrate the music and the weather with his hands, as PAUL and LEAH stand before the preacher. Once married, they kiss deeply: the preacher departs, and Paul and Leah mingle with their friends.

Falling Man fades the music out as one of the guests—a tall, stocky, heavily bearded young man–holds up a Mason jar filled with wine and taps it with a spoon.

DAMIEN: I'd like to propose a toast!

The group draws closer, surrounding Leah and Paul. They all pick up jars, and pass around bottles of open wine.

DAMIEN, *holding up a bottle:* Your first vintage–*he gestures toward Leah's belly*–and your first baby. And as your best man, Paul–and I AM your best man– I would like to wish you and your exquisite bride a very long, and very happy, life together.

Paul and Leah embrace; their friends applaud and raise their glasses.

DAMIEN: Wait! Wait–I have more to say—

The group groans.

WEDDING GUEST ONE: You're not going to talk all night, are you Damien? We love you but–

WEDDING GUEST TWO: Yeah, Damien–we all know how much you like to talk.

PAUL: Come on you guys–what did he say last year? Seven words?

The group laughs again–so does Damien. Then they become very silent, waiting for him to speak.

DAMIEN: This is an important time for you, Leah, and you, Paul–and for us, too–for all of us. All the work that's brought us to this place together. The planting of the vines, the restoration of the soil, the amazing regenerative capacities of the earth, in this place–

WEDDING GUEST ONE, *raising a glass:* It is amazing–

WEDDING GUEST TWO: A piece of paradise–

DAMIEN: It's...what you've done...what we've done...it's...it's given me hope. *Damien tears up, then regains his composure.* I remember how bitter I was–when we first met. Everything seemed so pointless to me–the materialism of the culture, my parent's constant refrain–get a job! get a job!

The group nods in recognition.

DAMIEN: And then I met you, Paul. And I was blown away by the possibilities of permaculture. I fell in love with working with my hands–with the skill and the intelligence involved in creating gardens, and in building houses and barns, and in crafting food...

WEDDING GUEST THREE: And you fell in love with the intelligence of crafting good ales and good wines!

GROUP: Good ales! Good wines!

The group toasts, laughs, nods.

DAMIEN: There is so much I've learned since we first met...you two opened a world to me...you taught me the value of learning the names of the plants and the names of the other species that coexist–that try to coexist–with us...

WEDDING GUEST ONE: Charina Bottae!

GROUP: Rubber boa!

WEDDING GUEST TWO: Phalocrocorax Carbo!

GROUP: Giant cormorant!

WEDDING GUEST THREE: Tegenaria Agrestis!

The group groans–then laughs.

DAMIEN: OK, OK, I know...I wasn't the best student in the world, but... well, it made an impression. It changed my life. *Damien pauses.* It gave me my life. I'll never forget–

WEDDING GUEST FOUR: Come on Damien! Enough already!

LEAH: Shussh–

DAMIEN: I'll never forget...the first time I went out to the farm–at school– and you were both just back from Ecuador–and Leah–you were showing those little kids how to tell time by the sun–and Paul–you had a chicken under each arm...and you both looked so happy...so ALIVE...and things just...well...it just...it just blew me away. That there really could be some meaning to my life, that I wasn't doomed to rot in the cube farm.

The group applauds.

WEDDING GUEST ONE: It blew you away all right–all the way to Tibet!

WEDDING GUEST TWO: And now, you're the yak cheese genius of north America!

GROUP: Yak cheese! Yak milk!

WEDDING GUEST THREE: Fermented yak milk! Served warm.

The group groans.

DAMIEN: Hey...it's an acquired taste. *He starts to tear up again.* What I'm trying to say, Leah, Paul...is that...over the years, you've been a major part of my...of...of my personal renaissance. And I know that's true for a lot of other people as well...and what I want–what I hope–for– for you, for us, all of us–is that your baby–the first baby of any of us– should grow up in a human ecosystem as rich as what we've created here...for these vines, and for each other...and for this community.

The group applauds: one of them picks up the guitar and starts to play. Damien raises his hand again.

DAMIEN: One more thing! Real quick–

Damien reaches behind the table, and pulls out a red lacquered box. It is covered with ornate lettering, and appears to be quite old. Damien hands the box to Paul and Leah. They open it: inside are six earthen balls, arranged in two rows, like ornaments.

LEAH: Oh, Damien.

PAUL: Seed bombs. Dame?

DAMIEN: I've been waiting a while to give you these. They're from a place outside Lhasa–from a farmer there...he–as I understood it, he got them from his father, who–somehow–smuggled them out of one of the monastery gardens during...before...I don't know the entire story...but the plants they're from were ancient. That's all I know—so much has been lost there...but I thought—that—well, some day, maybe ...you'll have just the place for them...and...well... Congratulations, Paul and Leah.

LEAH: Oh Damien.

DAMIEN, *holding up his glass:* To regeneration.

GROUP: To regeneration.

DAMIEN: And to life—to you, Leah and Paul.

GROUP: To life! To Leah and Paul!

The guitarist begins playing; Leah and Paul dance, as their friends continue to celebrate. Falling Man raises his hands and the vineyard fades away.

ANDREW: Spirit...I think I understand...you are showing me that Leah and Paul are working on perma...nature...uh, whatever that is that Leah called it. Well, that's wonderful. That's really wonderful.

Falling Man shakes his head, and gestures for Andrew to listen. In the air, the Chaconne becomes audible again and the voices of a cacophony of newscasters can be heard ...gradually their volume increases until they form a mosaic with the music.

Falling Man continues to use his hands and his body to tune into and mix the sounds. The stars and the clouds wheel overhead again...the days, nights, and seasons pass...and then, the color of sky begins to change, becoming a sickly yellow-brown.

VOICE MOSAIC: This morning, in the wake of yet another 8.2 magnitude earthquake off the coast of Japan, experts say the Fukushima nuclear power facility has again been severely damaged...In the wake of this latest calamity, TEPCO and the Japanese government are struggling to manage the scale of the disaster...Eyewitnesses say the frozen soil walls intended to contain radioactive water have failed, and people are fleeing the vicinity...A growing cloud of dust and fallout is visible from a distance and it is uncertain whether the area is safe for any human activity...There are unconfirmed reports of the beginning of a mass exodus from Japan, as people seek to escape the radiation... Experts say it is unclear, given the scale of the damage, whether there will be any attempt to further decommission the reactors...

ANDREW: What? You can't just abandon nuclear reactors! Nobody would do that.

Falling Man holds his hand out to silence Andrew, then he turns to bring the music volume and the wind up, and to mix more newscaster voices together as the days and nights whirl past—stars and sunlight, stars and sunlight, clouds, blue sky...

VOICE MOSAIC: Closer to home, experts say that residents along the western coast of North America do not need to worry about radiation exposure as the ocean and the distance will dilute any radiation to safe levels...Authorities claim that reports of dead sea-lions lining the California coast are isolated incidents, and biologists believe they died of natural causes...At this time, the governors of California, Oregon, and Washington have issued a statement reassuring residents that they will continue to monitor conditions...

ANDREW: That's ridiculous! The engineers know those reactors have to be shut down. And they will shut them down, Spirit.

Andrew lets go of his chair, and begins to pace.

ANDREW, *to himself:* I mean...no one with any knowledge would let fuel rods overheat. You have to keep them cool—it's not an option. Burning fuel...that...that...that would be really bad.

Andrew becomes dizzy and leans again on the chair.

Falling Man gestures for Andrew to stop talking, as the sky darkens ominously, followed by the sound of heavy rain and another newscaster voice mosaic.

VOICE MOSAIC: In the wake of unprecedented storms along the entire West Coast, massive landslides have left tens of thousands homeless...In response to public concerns over whether the rain might be radioactive, experts say there is no need for alarm...Citing ongoing budget disputes, the California legislature has announced an indefinite cessation of operations due to lack of funds...Budget impasses make the timeline for landslide cleanup uncertain, as thousands continue to live without electricity or basic plumbing...

Falling Man stops the rain and fades the voice mosaic as the sun flickers through a dirty brown haze. As the Chaconne continues, shadows of people begin to pass all around Falling Man and Andrew, as if a mass migration is underway. Falling Man brings up another voice mosaic.

VOICE MOSAIC: Throughout the interior of the United States and Canada, severe drought continues to damage crops, kill livestock, and destroy livelihoods...Experts say the Pioneer Canyon wildfire has now consumed more than 90 million acres of forest and grassland, and officials say the end is nowhere in sight...Due to additional budget cutbacks, all Idaho schools and state/municipal offices will be closed until further notice...In yet another casualty of this year's fire season, the Wyoming legislature recently declared bankruptcy, claiming environmental disasters and lack of federal funding have left the state unable to provide even the most basic services...

ANDREW, *becoming irritated:* Fear mongering! What are you trying to show me, Spirit? That our leaders sat around and argued while everything burned to the ground or slid into the ocean? I don't believe it. People on the West Coast are always carrying on about the end of the world. It's a scam to scare people, and to stay in control...to get more money for their political agenda.

Still leaning on the chair for balance, Andrew turns and moves away from Falling Man.

ANDREW: I hate all this emotional crap. Give me facts and data–things we can deal with. Problems we can solve...In the end, cooler heads will prevail. They have to. They always do.

Falling Man looks mutely at Andrew and uses his hands to slow down the rotation of the earth, as the light turns a pale greenish yellow. The Chaconne fades, barely audible.

VOICE MOSAIC: This just in: a 7.7 magnitude earthquake has been reported in Seattle...In an unprecedented event, a major fault beneath the Strait of Juan de Fuca appears to have unzipped–a phenomenon long dreaded by geologists...Landforms around Victoria, British Columbia have apparently collapsed into the Strait...A chain reaction of earthquakes appears to have taken place all along the West Coast...We appear to have lost power and communication with a large number of our affiliates...In the wake of a 6.7 aftershock, the San Onofre nuclear power plant has been damaged: eyewitness reports are that parts of the structure have blown off...Current radiation levels appear to be safe, though residents with thyroid problems are encouraged to leave the area...

ANDREW: Stop, Spirit, stop! We have made mistakes, granted, and OK, sometimes we build in stupid places–that's nothing new...but don't you think you're being a little extreme? And besides...even if this were true...what am I supposed to do about it? What's it got to do with me?

In response, Falling Man shapes his hands again, and the voices and music fade: Andrew and Falling Man are standing in the interior of an old, simple house. There is a large crack in the wall between the windows and the ceiling; it is dark outside, and an oil lamp is on the kitchen table, burning.

Leah is sitting at the table, holding a sleeping baby. Her head is wrapped in a scarf, and it is clear that all her hair has fallen out; a 5-year old child is playing with toys on the floor by her feet.

Leah is very pale and very thin. Paul is also very thin; he is stacking small rounds of wood next to a cast iron stove. When he finishes, he comes to sit at the table with Leah. She sits with her eyes closed—clearly very tired.

PAUL: Let me take Shelby, Leah.

LEAH: Just one more minute.

PAUL: Leah.

LEAH: Yes. I know.

Leah hands Paul the baby. Paul puts her down on a small cot in the corner, then returns to the table.

LEAH: Did Damien get the goats?

PAUL: Yes. He just left.

LEAH: And what about the chickens?

PAUL: Leah. We have to leave them.

5-YEAR OLD BEN: Dad?

PAUL: Yes, Ben?

5-YEAR OLD BEN: Will you play with me?

ANDREW, *to himself*: He looks just like my Ben did—at that age.

PAUL: Not right now. I need to talk to Momma.

Paul reaches across the table to hold Leah's hand. She continues to sit with her eyes closed.

LEAH: I love this house.

PAUL: I know.

LEAH: I love the vineyard.

PAUL: I know.

LEAH: And the trees. The sunlight and the shadows.

PAUL: I know.

LEAH: I don't want to leave.

PAUL: I know.

LEAH: I'm really tired, Paul.

PAUL: I know.

LEAH: What's going to happen to you and the kids?

PAUL: Leah, don't.

LEAH: Paul.

PAUL: Don't worry, Leah. We'll be fine.

LEAH: You know what I mean.

PAUL: Don't worry about it, Leah.

LEAH: Paul.

PAUL: We don't need to talk about this anymore–

LEAH: Paul.

PAUL: Leah. It's our only option–

LEAH: Robert isn't well.

PAUL: I know.

LEAH: And my mother–she–

PAUL: Leah. You know we have to go. Before the kids get sick too–

LEAH: I know.

PAUL: Please stop worrying. I promise you...I'll figure it out. I'll figure something out. Just–just not right now, OK? Not right now.

Leah appears to have fallen asleep in her chair. Paul continues to hold her hand across the table: he lays his other arm on the table, and rests his head on it.

Falling Man raises his hands and the Chaconne becomes audible again: as the music grows louder, Leah and Paul's home fades into shadow and Andrew and Falling Man are again alone.

Andrew lets go of his chair and begins to pace as Falling Man again makes the stars begin to swirl–this time much more slowly.

ANDREW, *to himself*: I mean, I know I'm in a dream, right? This is just a dream. It's a bad dream. *Andrew turns to look at Falling Man.* And besides–there's still the East Coast, right? They can go there. Things are better there. Leah can get help there.

Falling Man's gestures are sharper now and sadder. Jaw tensed, he brings the music up louder, along with another voice mosaic.

VOICE MOSAIC: As another Category 6 hurricane bears down on the East Coast, residents are advised to move inland...In the Central and South-Central United States, a series of massive derechos have decimated the power grid, cutting off the electricity to more than 60 million people...

ANDREW: Category 6? There's no such thing–is there?

The light becomes very bright and a hot steady wind begins to blow.

VOICE MOSAIC: For the third year in a row, the record heat wave has destroyed most of the Midwest grain crop...National food reserves are nearly depleted, according to...After yet another deadlocked week with no resolution in sight, Congress has declared yet another government shutdown...

Young people with hooded sweatshirts run past Andrew and Falling Man. Someone throws a Molotov cocktail: it shatters and bursts into flames at Andrew's feet. Car alarms, the sounds of breaking glass, and screams are mixed with the music and voice mosaic.

VOICE MOSAIC: Riots broke out following the disclosure that additional tax breaks for the wealthy were to be paired with a slashing of food aid for the unemployed...Across the country, people mobbed local grocery stores, overwhelming police lines and clearing shelves in less than an hour...Stocks plunged to a new low today on Wall Street, dipping below 5000 after investors took their profits on concerns that corporate taxes might go up, reducing shareholders' gains...

Falling Man crouches low to the ground, as he and Andrew are surrounded by flashing police lights, mixed with the blue hue of television screens, the intense neon of Times Square and Tokyo, and the orange sky glow of industrial developments. The hum of fluorescent ballast can be heard, welling up like a monstrous hive of insects, drowning out the Chaconne.

From low to the ground, Falling Man generates another voice mosaic.

VOICE MOSAIC: According to the latest report, two of the Alabama reactors may have been affected by prolonged loss of power caused by the derechos...In the wake of the latest hurricane, police and first responder services in the most hard hit areas are non-existent...Throughout the Gulf Coast region, it remains to be seen whether funding for essential services will be restored...

ANDREW: Oh wait–wait. I think I'm starting to get it. This is about the lifeboats, right? Getting into the lifeboats. *His demeanor brightens.* I'm supposed to help Paul and Leah get into their lifeboat.

Falling Man shrugs. Protestors dressed as sea turtles, trees, and butterflies, and carrying signs saying "HELL NO GMO" and "FEED THE POOR, STARVE THE RICH" pass by.

Falling Man mixes another voice mosaic with the Chaconne.

VOICE MOSAIC: In midst of crop failures worldwide, protestors claim genetically modified seeds and pesticides are responsible...Corporate lawyers are demanding gag orders on anyone suggesting the public has the right to refuse genetically modified crops or food...

ANDREW, *emphatically:* I get it. I get it. Their farm. I'm supposed to help them with their farm.

Falling Man shakes his head, as the music takes on a more desperate and out of control feel.

VOICE MOSAIC: Across the globe, economic collapse has people moving into the streets...Extreme swings in global weather again this season have made it nearly impossible for farmers to plant...Worldwide, farmer suicides have reached epidemic proportions as...Extreme temperatures have melted pavement and killed thousands in urban areas throughout Europe, Africa, and the Middle East, however experts say normal temperatures will return soon...

ANDREW: Why are you shaking your head, Spirit?

Falling Man turns away.

VOICE MOSAIC: Global food stocks are depleted…The recent collapse of the U.S. bond markets, and the fickle attitude of currency traders means it is almost impossible to import grain...Refugee camps have been established throughout the East Coast, to deal with the massive influx of people who are unemployed and without shelter...As winter approaches, people are urged to aid those in need...

ANDREW: Wait. What is it? I get it, I'm telling you. I get it. Why won't you stop?

With very great effort, Falling Man manages to bring up the music and make the sky swirl again. As the days and nights begin to pass in sequence, the clouds flatten out and the sky turns a dull gray.

Falling Man slows the motion of the earth and brings up the wind, which blows away the haze. Chest heaving from the effort, Falling Man looks up again at the sky, which is once again a clear blue.

A white unmarked jet appears high overhead: as it passes, it leaves a trail behind it. A moment later, another unmarked jet appears, moving in the opposite direction. Also leaving a trail, the second jet passes over the trail of the first, forming a large X. A third jet appears: it traces a U shape between the points of the X, then returns in the same direction from which it came.

Andrew and Falling Man watch as the trails spread across the sky, obscuring the blue sky beneath another flat gray haze.

ANDREW, *to himself:* Oh come on. Chemtrails? Even Leah wouldn't–

Falling Man gestures to Andrew to stop talking, and he brings up another voice mosaic. A hot wind begins to blow again.

VOICE MOSAIC: In the wake of a decade of record-setting global temperature increases, experts suggest weather modification may be our last chance to...The rapid melting of the Greenland and Antarctic Ice Sheets has forced climatologists to consider something known as geo-engineering...Policymakers state that moderating the weather would enable us to grow enough food to address global famine and instability...Also known as Solar Radiation Management or SRM, experts say the process is safe and effective...By dispersing small particles into the atmosphere, we can cheaply and effectively...

ANDREW: No no no no–look Spirit–I'll be the first to admit we've made a mess of it–but whole scale spraying of the atmosphere? Would they really do that?

Falling Man continues to orchestrate more voices, and to make the stars swirl again.

VOICE MOSAIC: In response to public concerns regarding long term effects of SRM, experts say there is nothing to worry about...At the global emergency summit, technology experts and world leaders have agreed that geo-engineering may be our last, best hope for regaining environmental, social, and economic stabilization across the planet... Perhaps most encouraging, budget analysts say the costs are relatively minimal...

ANDREW: The costs! That's absurd! What about the unintended consequences? I don't know which is more arrogant: to think we caused the planet to warm...or to think that we can stop it!

Falling Man quiets the music and brings the daylight up on a refugee camp market stall. The stall is roofed with blue tarps: near the back are living quarters, sided with stained plywood and separated from the front of the stall by old blankets.

The alley in front of the stall is lined with junk: rusty bicycles, old cans, and stacks of cardboard. In the distance stands the Washington Monument–its top broken off and surrounded by rubble.

SHELBY GOODRICH and her brother BEN are trying to hang a set of lights on the outside of the stall. Next to Shelby and Ben, an old woman with frizzy grey hair is sitting on a stool, potting plants.

Beside the old woman, on a piece of scrap plywood, is a hand-drawn message. It reads "HERBS: DANDELION, BURDOCK, THISTLE" HEAL THE SOIL! GMO FREE! ALUMINUM RESISTANT!

ANDREW, *incredulous:* Is that my sister Andrea? Selling weeds in pots? On the Washington Mall? *Whispering, to himself:* I don't believe it.

Falling Man gestures to Andrew to be silent.

BEN: Is this where you want the lights, Grandma?

SHELBY: I think we should try to hang them on a tree.

BEN: We don't have a tree, Shelby.

SHELBY: We could try to find one. An old branch or something. Or we could make one out of wire.

BEN: Great idea–we'll celebrate Winter Solstice with a remnant of industrial culture–electric lights and a metal tree.

ANDREA: Ben, don't be so cynical. At least we have electricity this year.

BEN: That's right–we do. So we can see the dirt floor better.

ANDREA, *sighing:* Stop, Ben. Shelby...why don't you look in the trunk and see if you can find something we can decorate with? I think there might be some ribbons in there. You're not going out to look for a tree, or a branch. The camp isn't very safe right now.

Shelby goes into the back of the tent and begins looking through a large trunk.

BEN: When was this camp ever safe, Grandma?

ANDREA: Well...when the UN first came in, it was safe. They did a good job keeping order...but then...

BEN: Well now all the police are thugs. Fucking thugs. They kicked the shit out of Randall's brother last week. Said he'd stolen canned beans from the storage. Then they took all his ration cards.

SHELBY, *from the back of the tent:* Do you think we'll ever get out of here, Grandma?

ANDREA: I don't know Shelby. I don't know what's going to happen. At least we can eat. That's good.

BEN: God, Grandma–did you always think so small?

SHELBY: Ben!

BEN: How can you be such an asskiss, Shelby?

ANDREA, *sighing*: Ben!

BEN: Grandma, I think we need to try to get out of here...head up north somewhere.

ANDREA: Oh Ben...I'm too old for that sort of thing.

BEN: Grandma, I can't stay here much longer. I can't stand this. We're treated like criminals...and we haven't done anything. Jared's parents said the drone strikes could start again, any time. They're already happening in Maryland.

ANDREA: It's not a permanent situation–we've just got to be patient.

BEN: You always say that–but we've been here almost 3 years now. Living in this fucking tent.

ANDREA: Give it a little more time, Ben.

BEN: Why should I?

Shelby finds an ornate box in the trunk. She carries it to the front of the tent.

SHELBY: Look what I found. I think it's an ornament box!

Shelby opens the box, and her expression changes from hopeful to confused.

SHELBY: Grandma...what are these?

Andrea examines the brown orbs nestled inside the box.

ANDREA: Oh...those belonged to your mother–to your parents.

Ben and Shelby each pick one up.

ANDREA: They were a wedding present, I think–from one of their friends.

SHELBY: But what are they?

ANDREA: They're seed bombs.

SHELBY: Seed bombs?

BEN: Sweet–weapons!

ANDREA, *sighing*: No, Ben. Shelby, they were a permaculture thing... at one point–all over the U.S.–the roads–we were so oil addicted, at least that is over–it really was insane–everyone was driving constantly ...and the native landscapes were in really bad shape.

SHELBY: We learned about that in school! People drove for hours–one person in a car–

ANDREA: Yes, Shelby–and it wasn't that long ago. And we'd still be doing it...if we could. *Andrea's voice becomes distant.* What the permaculture people would do is make seed bombs–out of native plants that were either completely gone or only surviving in patchwork–and they would throw them out from cars, trains, bikes, into vacant lots and median strips and other areas where they might have a chance to take root again.

SHELBY: Why?

ANDREA: Because they were trying to make things better. They were trying to restore the ecosystems.

BEN: Yeah. They were trying to stop Fukushima with plants.

ANDREA: No, Ben–nobody could stop that, once it really got going.

BEN: Yeah–once it *really* got going. Too late. Sorry we fucked your generation. Oops.

SHELBY: Ben–it's not Grandma's fault.

BEN: Then whose fault is it? Nobody's ever responsible…what's up with that shit?

ANDREA: Your parents were trying to make a small difference, in a way that mattered to them.

SHELBY: My parents were doing this? Throwing seed bombs?

ANDREA: I don't know. I suppose so. They really loved working on the land, Shelby. And your dad–he really knew how to make a bottle of wine.

BEN: Yeah, Shel, that's why they named you after a tree. "The willow growing by the water we use to make wine."

SHELBY, *studying a seed bomb*: These are really beautiful. What kinds of plants are in them? Do you know?

ANDREA: I don't know. I think they came from Tibet. I'm pretty sure it was the friend who owned the yak farm who gave them to your parents.

SHELBY: What's a yak?

BEN: A cow, Shel. A cow with a lot of hair.

SHELBY: Wow. Yaks. Seed bombs. *She tosses the seed bomb lightly, then catches it again.* Do you think they'll grow? If we throw them?

BEN: Shel, nothing grows now—all the aluminum in the soil from the dumbass geoengineers—

ANDREA, *sighing:* Ben—stop. Shelby—they wouldn't grow here...but maybe somewhere, someday, they will.

SHELBY: Wow. Grandma, I'm going to hang them up, OK? With the ribbons. They'll be our solstice ornaments.

ANDREA: That's nice, Shelby. I like that idea.

Falling Man moves his hands and the Chaconne becomes audible again. The tent city fades into the shadows, the sky grows dark, and once again, stars wheel overhead.

ANDREW: OK. OK. I get it. I get it. But you need to understand something Spirit...I'm an engineer...and I know we can solve these problems. I know we can. I just hate all that doom and gloom shit. We'll find solutions...we just...we just...we just need more time.

Falling man looks sadly at Andrew and brings up another voice mosaic. As the voices weave over one another, the stars and the earth slow, then start to turn in reverse, as if time is moving backwards.

Police in heavy riot gear begin to move rapidly past Andrew and Falling Man.

VOICE MOSAIC: Across the globe, reports of a total bee collapse have horticulturists in a panic...Experts suspect that genetically modified crops and pesticide use are responsible...Meanwhile, a new corporate strain of seed has been introduced, over the protests of people across the globe...To protect the intellectual property rights of seed owners, all seed saving has been banned worldwide...The owners of private greenhouse enclaves have organized to protect their property, claiming that vandals have repeatedly stormed the gates, attempting to steal...And while the climate change debate continues, the trade group Industrialists for a Powerful Future is busy mapping out ways to drill for oil in the new passage through the formerly ice-blocked areas of northern Canada...

ANDREW: Spirit—what are you saying?

Falling Man takes Andrew's chair and sits down backwards on it. He covers his face with one hand, while with the other, he continues to animate the future through voice mosaic and sound.

ANDREW: What? That I finally figured it out, but it's too late?

A hot wind begins to blow again, accompanied by a keening sound, as if the atmosphere is slowly leaking away.

VOICE MOSAIC: There are reports of methane plumes being released from underneath the permafrost, bubbling up from the ocean floor all across the Arctic...Experts say the last of the coral reef has died along the coast of Australia...Cancer rates have skyrocketed worldwide, particularly along coastal regions, where shellfish and seafood appear to be uniformly contaminated with high levels of radioactive isotopes ...While some scientists assert that data shows we are in the midst of the sixth great species extinction, others say this is untrue and...

ANDREW: Spirit—look. We can fix this.

Falling Man shakes his head.

VOICE MOSAIC: As the ice caps continue to rapidly melt, the conveyer currents are slowing dramatically, causing the oceans to become anaerobic...Massive fish die-offs suggest that the Earth's oceans are becoming dangerously deoxygenated...a condition hypothesized as a Canfield Ocean...

The buzzing of drones is heard overhead.

ANDREW: Wait a minute—I know that sound.

The buzzing sound grows louder. Lights flash, followed by an explosion. Andrew crouches, covering his ears.

ANDREW: No Spirit! No!

The bombing stops. For a moment it is completely silent and dark.

Slowly, Falling Man rises from the chair. As he stands, the moon rises into the sky behind him: its light illuminates Ben, who is now sitting—head down, knees up—in the smoking rubble of his grandmother's refugee tent, his sister's still body lying beside him.

ANDREW: No! No! They're children! They're children!

CAMP POLICE, *over a radio:* We're in pursuit now.

DISPATCH: Location?

CAMP POLICE: Washington Mall. Sector 7.

ANDREW: NO!

A single, blinding beam of light hits Ben, who stands up, his hands in front of his eyes. His shirt is covered with blood. He is still holding a seed bomb.

CAMP POLICE: Move toward the light! Move toward the light!

Ben winds up and hurls the seed bomb at the police. Falling Man throws out his arms in an attempt to turn up the volume of the Chaconne—but he cannot drown out the patter of the automatic weapons. In the wake of bullet spray, Falling Man strikes Andrew's chair, sending it reeling: as it slams into the ground, shattering, the refugee camp disappears, leaving Andrew and Falling Man alone again.

ANDREW, *sobbing as he crumples to the ground:* No! No! No!

With great effort, Falling Man makes the stars wheel overhead again. As he does, Andrew's penthouse reappears. Where the elevator once stood, there is now a smoldering pile of rubble. Blood is splattered on the wall nearby, and all that remains of the French doors is a gaping hole through which the Washington Monument–now glowing a dark, incandescent red–can be seen. In the midst of the destruction, the dining table still stands–battered and burned, but intact.

Falling Man crosses the room and jumps up onto the table. He turns to look back at Andrew–who continues to lie sobbing on the floor.

ANDREW: This can't happen. This can't happen. This can't happen.

Falling Man stands on the edge of the table, with his heels hanging over and his arms away from his sides–as if he is preparing for a dive. As the final notes of the Chaconne sound overhead, Falling Man crouches, then springs up and back, into a slow, perfect, reverse swan dive. The sound of a diving board spring echoes through the air, and Andrew's penthouse—and everything in his world–disappears into darkness.

Morning Arrives

It is 6 a.m. The sky is a pale, cloudless blue, and the early morning light is dancing across the Washington Monument, bathing it in tones of pink and yellow.

As the sun begins to crest the horizon, its rays stream in through the French doors of Andrew's master suite, illuminating the austere beauty of the room, and forming a golden patchwork across the bed. Everything is in order: Andrew's robe is neatly draped across the foot of his bed, and his socks are carefully folded atop the bureau.

The sun rises higher in the sky, and its rays come to rest upon Andrew's arm, trailing out from beneath the bedclothes and hanging over the edge of the mattress. On the nightstand, there is an empty pill bottle; on the floor, there is another.

As the sun's rays strike his bureau, Andrew's phone begins to ring.

Andrew does not stir, and the phone continues to ring and ring, unanswered.

About the Author

Deirdre Duffy is an ecological design practitioner.

She lives in the Cascadia bioregion.

For more information about her, visit www.divergentink.com.

Photo: Isabel Gates.